W9-BSM-610

COUNTRY DARK

Also by Chris Offutt

Kentucky Straight
The Same River Twice
The Good Brother
Out of the Woods
No Heroes: A Memoir of Coming Home
My Father, the Pornographer

COUNTRY DARK

CHRIS OFFUTT

Grove Press
New York

FIRST EDITION

Published simultaneously in Canada
Printed in the United States of America

Text Design by Norman Tuttle
This book was set in Bembo by
Alpha Design & Composition of Pittsfield, NH

First Grove Atlantic hardcover edition: April 2018

Library of Congress Cataloging-in-Publication data available for this title.

ISBN 978-0-8021-2779-2
eISBN 978-0-8021-4616-8

Grove Press
an imprint of Grove Atlantic
154 West 14th Street
New York, NY 10011

Distributed by Publishers Group West

groveatlantic.com

18 19 20 21 10 9 8 7 6 5 4 3 2 1

For Melissa Allee Ginsburg

I returned home to my family, with a determination to bring them as soon as possible to live in Kentucky, which I esteemed a second paradise, at the risk of my life and fortune.

—Daniel Boone

1954

Chapter One

Tucker had been walking for six hours through early morning ground fog that rose in shimmering waves. One vehicle passed him, a farmer with a load of firewood, two sullen kids, and a skinny wife holding a baby. Tucker knew they wouldn't pick him up. He didn't blame the baleful driver, a hat twisted on his head to deflect the sun, a cigarette clamped between his teeth. Poor guy had enough to worry about.

Tucker sought shade and found a strip cast from the leg of a billboard encouraging him to buy shaving cream. He needed a shave, but didn't figure a giant picture would convince him to spend money on something he could make from borax, oil, and chipped soap. He dropped his rucksack, opened a can of Libby's Vienna sausages and ate them with saltine crackers. He used a church key to open a bottle of Ale-8, and drank half.

A katydid landed on his forearm and he admired its silky green body, serrated back legs, and delicate wings. They were prettier than a grasshopper and didn't piss all over you like frogs did. The insect leaned backward and swelled itself, the thorax expanding, wings distending as if preparing for battle. Tucker nudged it away. He dropped the empty sausage can in a ditch blooming with milkweed and set off walking.

The sun was rising high in the sky. He needed to find more shade, sufficient enough for a nap. Instead, he caught a ride with a World War II veteran driving an old '39 coupe. The man didn't say a word for ninety miles, but dropped Tucker at the Ripley Bridge. He thanked the driver, who grunted, spat out the window, and drove away.

Tucker stood in Ohio and looked across the river at the swollen green land of Kentucky. He'd left in early summer and returned in spring, a winter of war in between. He began crossing the bridge. Wind made it sway and he grabbed a strut. Briefly he recalled seeing a dozen dead enemy strewn about a dynamited bridge near the front, a boundary that changed week to week. If Ohio attacked Kentucky, one bunch or the other would blow this bridge to smithereens. Anyone who fought wouldn't know the difference between soldiers, the same as North and South Koreans. It was Truman's war, not Tucker's, but he'd killed and nearly been killed and watched men tremble with fear and cry like kids. His army pay of four hundred forty dollars was folded tight and distributed about his body in every pocket. The eleven medals he received were at the bottom of his rucksack.

He walked across the bridge and set foot on the soil he'd desperately missed. Beneath a willow grown fat from proximity to water, he used his thumbnail to split a wooden match in half, saving the other half, and lit a Lucky, reclining his head on his ruck. The swaying willow fronds scattered light and shade in a kaleidoscopic pattern that gently lulled him to sleep.

Tucker awoke from dreamless rest, quickly alert, then relaxed as the knowledge of his whereabouts seeped through his mind. He lit another Lucky. He blew a smoke ring that dissipated as if struck by a hammer. The steeple of a church rose above the tree line and he knew a town was ahead but not the name of the town or which county he was in. It didn't matter. He didn't like towns—too many people doing too many things at once, and everything boring with its repetition and noise. He wondered vaguely what day it was, what month.

Tucker drank from his canteen and headed east. Walking soothed him. He enjoyed putting his legs to work like a machine he oversaw, the ruck's weight on his back, the familiar strain tugging his shoulders. Out of habit he kept shifting his weight to accommodate the rifle that wasn't there. The lack of a weapon troubled him in a distant way, like an amputee who'd lost a limb.

He'd grown up with guns as common as shovels, but had felt a genuine affection for the M1 carbine. As the shortest and youngest member of his platoon, he rarely spoke. His first words were in response to a corporal asking how he liked his rifle. Tucker had said, "Shoots good," and a silence fell over the other men as sudden as a net. They looked at one another, then began laughing in an uproarious manner. Four died in combat and would never laugh at him again.

He heard the rattle of an engine hitting on five cylinders, the sound like a dog with a limp. He stepped onto the grass to let a pickup go by. One tailgate chain was missing. The bumper showed daylight in rust holes, and an Ohio license plate was held in place by baling wire. The truck slowed, matching Tucker's pace, the driver keeping the motor alive while yelling out the window.

"You needing a ride?"

Tucker nodded.

"Well get on in, then. I can't stop or it might not start again."

The driver leaned across the bench seat and shoved the passenger door open. It swung out, reached the limit of its twin hinges, and swung back shut.

"Damn door," the driver said. "Come on if you've a mind to."

Tucker continued walking as he looked the truck over, a 1949 Chevrolet with a painted grill, dented sides, and a bed slightly askew from bad leaf shocks. In one smooth motion he stepped onto the rusty running board, opened the door, and slid onto the cracked leather bench seat. The suddenness of his arrival startled the driver. The truck veered momentarily but he straightened its progress and they went a few miles in silence save for the clanking engine, a sound that began to annoy Tucker, who didn't understand how anyone could neglect a machine that needed maintenance. Sunlight glared along the river, its surface shiny as lard.

The driver tensed his left arm against the steady pull of badly aligned tires. The truck belonged to his brother-in-law, pretty much a nitwit who kept a lit cigarette lodged in a gap where he'd lost a tooth. Bolted to the dashboard was a coffee can filled with sand and cigarette butts.

The driver inspected his passenger with quick sidelong glances. The boy had short clipped hair and wore russet-colored boots laced up the front. An army shirt had a red stop sign patch with some kind of dragon embroidered in gold. He was probably wearing his older brother's fatigue shirt out of a sense of honor, or maybe just no money for better. Families on the Kentucky side of the river didn't have a pot to piss in or a window to throw it out of.

"You hunting work?" the driver said.

Tucker shook his head.

"If you're wanting a tailor-made, dig around in that coffee can. Enough ends in there to build one."

Tucker looked out the window. He'd spent hours in transport vehicles beside men who liked to talk, and learned to ignore them by concentrating on the passing terrain. The truck's momentum swept the translucent bulbs of dandelions into miniature whirlwinds. Tucker wondered vaguely how far a dandelion seed could drift on a breeze, if all the dandelions in the world had a common grandfather. The truck door rattled loose in its latch. A nuthatch walked headfirst down a hickory and Tucker recalled trying to duplicate that feat as a kid. He'd fallen six times, then quit. It was his favorite bird, a fact he kept to himself. Children had favorite birds and women favored certain pets. In a pinch, a man might like a horse.

"Got in a fight with my wife," the driver said. "Had to get out of the house, off the porch, and away from the yard. Hell, it was so bad I left the damn state! She gets in these moods, starts slamming cabinet doors and banging skillets. Got to head for cover. Her brother lives across the street and I took his rig. He's about useless. You like it? I don't. Runs rough, but I can push it like a borrowed mule. Which it is if you think about it, right?"

Tucker nodded. Now that he was nearly eighteen with some veteran's pay, he'd be in the market for a wife himself. But not a town woman, and damn sure not one from Ohio.

"A man's got to be free, don't he," the driver said. "Shit fire and save matches, that's my name, ain't it. I'm Tom Freeman. Free's right there in my handle. I can't help it, I was born to it. But I don't have to tell you about free, you out roaming the roads big as day. You ain't a runaway, are you? They say juvenile delinquents are tearing this country to pieces like picking a chicken. Comic books is what it is. You don't read them do you?"

Tucker shook his head. Comic books cost a dime, a nickel if the covers were torn off, and such sums were better reserved for necessary goods. Every cent he'd earned as a kid he gave to his mother, who used the money for food. She never purchased dry goods or notions and her kids didn't fool with comic books. When she died, Tucker enlisted. He'd received one letter overseas, the envelope crumpled, his sister's writing blurred on a scrap of brown paper bag, the information sad—his younger brother fell down a well and drowned.

"Tell me something," the driver said. "I ain't a-caring if you're on the run, I just don't want to get mixed up in another feller's trouble. What are you wearing them clothes with that dragon patch for? A body might think you're a chucklehead out playing army in the woods. That what you're up to? Slip off from the home place to act like a soldier?"

Tucker slowly turned his head, his shoulders and body following at a slower pace, until he unleashed his gaze on the driver. Freeman stopped talking as if a cork was plugged into a bottle. The boy's deep-set eyes were two different colors—one blue, the other brown. Freeman had heard about that with cats but never a human man.

"Griffin," Tucker said.

"Huh?"

"Ain't no dragon."

"Say it's some kind of griffith?"

Tucker nodded.

"What in the hell is that?"

Tucker shrugged and averted his head. Freeman felt a relief similar to watching his wife angrily turn away to end a conversation. He had begun his professional life carrying a portable grinder and helping his father as a door-to-door knife sharpener. His father kept a concealed pistol and a half pint of liquor, ready to woo or fight anyone who got briggity. Freeman did the same. He considered halting the truck and sending the boy away. But he had no desire to return to a tense home, and had been hoping for a drinking partner. This boy would have to do. After a few tastes of rotgut rye he'd loosen his tongue enough to tell Freeman what a damn griffith was.

The truck followed the river, and though it was out of sight beyond the heavy brush and trees, Tucker could smell the water. Sweat trickled inside his clothes. He was grateful for the heat, hoped never to be cold again after the Korean winter. He'd once lain in ambush so long that his clothing froze to the ground. Along the road, forsythia swayed in the ditch, its yellow blossoms pushed aside by the greening leaves. He should have kept on walking. He resolved to get out at the next crossroad. If ever compelled to travel in a vehicle again, he'd be the one driving. Until then Tucker remained vigilant for a turnoff. He'd jump out and stay away from people.

The road continued east, shifting south to circumvent bends in the river, entering patches shaded by maples. The truck slowed for a sharp turn and Tucker saw a water moccasin draped over the low boughs of a tree. Farther on, a possum scurried for safety. Freeman swerved toward it, laughing, but missed the animal. The boy had no reaction and Freeman began thinking something was seriously wrong with him. Briefly, he reconsidered the idea of funneling liquor into a lamebrain on the loose.

The road made three S-turns, then hit a straight stretch, and Freeman steered to a wide spot beneath an oak. He slipped the truck out of gear and goosed it with the foot feed, keeping a high idle. Tucker set his hand on the door handle.

"Hold your horses, Griffith," Freeman said. "Look here."

Freeman held a thirty-eight-caliber pistol loose in his hand, not in a particularly threatening manner, but the quarters were close. Tucker eased back against the seat, presenting the side of his body as a smaller target, protecting his vitals.

"Open that glove box up," Freeman said.

Slowly and with great care, Tucker pressed the button to release the trapdoor in the dashboard. It was rusty and stuck. Tucker shifted his thumb on the button but it wouldn't open.

"You got to give it a hard little rap with your knuckle," Freeman said.

Tucker struck the button and the glove box fell open. Inside were three sheets of S&H Green Stamps adhering to themselves, a packet of BC powder for headaches, a Zippo lighter, and a jar of clear liquid. Freeman gestured with the pistol.

"Reach that jar out," Freeman said.

Tucker lifted the pint jar, designed for canning vegetables in autumn. Freeman pressed the gun barrel against the griffin in the center of Tucker's 108th Airborne patch.

"Now," Freeman said. "Take you a little drink."

Tucker opened the lid, which emitted the sharp scent of corn liquor. He lifted the jar to his lips, watching the gun. His mouth immediately anesthetized itself and his throat began burning. Warmth spread from his torso along his limbs.

"One more," Freeman said. "Make it a good 'un."

Tucker drank, breathing through his nose, tears leaking down his face. Strength swept through him like weather, leaving him more clearheaded than before. He lowered the jar and waited.

Freeman looked close, wondering if the harsh liquor might have altered the color of the boy's eyes. He'd seen that before but the change usually ran to the red.

"Pretty good, ain't it," Freeman said. "Don't reckon you'd a took a drink without me holding a gun on you, would you?"

Tucker shook his head once, slowly. Freeman slid his finger from the trigger and offered the revolver.

"Now," Freeman said, grinning big, "you make me take a drink."

He began laughing, great guffaws that rose and fell as if rediscovering the source of merriment. It was a good joke, the best joke, and he'd played it well. Tucker's breathing was calm as a man asleep. Time had slowed, as if the world around him had doubled its pace. He'd felt this way in combat, a fish in the sea while all around him animals flailed to stay afloat. He took the pistol and aimed it at Freeman's head. His laughter halted abruptly. Tucker removed the keys from the ignition. The truck shuddered and the engine stopped. He stepped out of the cab, tossed the keys into the weeds, and shouldered his ruck.

"Don't follow me," Tucker said.

He back stepped into the woods still holding the moonshine and pistol. He walked a few hundred yards to an overhang of willow. He opened his ruck, tucked the jar in, and removed his Ka-Bar combat knife and strapped it to his belt. He headed south, having formulated a plan to find the Licking River and follow it home. Though tired, he walked five more miles away from the vehicle. He climbed to a high spot and ate some of his food. He lay on his back, knife at one side and Freeman's pistol by the other, watching night arrive.

Tucker had missed the sheer expanse of sky at night, the tiny cluster of seven sisters, Orion's sword, and the drinking gourd that aimed north. The moon was a gibbous, barely there, as if chewed away. The sky stretched black in every direction. Clouds blocked the stars, lending an unfathomable depth to the air. The tree line was gone and hilltops blended with the black tapestry of night. It was country dark. He closed his eyes, feeling safe.

Chapter Two

Tucker had lied about his age and enlisted eleven months before the Korean war ended. Everyone in the hills of home looked alike—short, thick, squinty-eyed, and strong. For the past year Tucker had lived and worked with people from off—Italians, Jews, Negroes, Poles, and Indians—and saw little difference beyond tint of skin and accent. They all missed home. The black soldiers tested him initially, trying to learn if he was a southern racist, but Tucker passed their reckonings and wound up preferring their company. They had grown up as poor as him, hunted the same game, lived separately from fancy people, and needed little in the way of resources. Strangest of all were the white soldiers who despised Tucker for buddying around with black men. It made no sense and strengthened his resolve to avoid people in general.

After specialist training at Fort Campbell, the most outstanding soldiers were mustered in formation. Tucker stood in the front row of the army's best recruits—marksmen, machine gunners, BAR men, close-combat experts, precision grenade throwers—all of them turned out in their BDUs under a sallow sun. They faced two officers: a colonel they'd never seen before and Major Buckner, a man they called a prick with ears. Buckner maintained a spit shine to his boots and bloused his trousers in a way that kept the sharp creases intact. Belted snugly beneath his chin was a strap holding a pristine wool hat with a polished visor. He carried a brass-tipped swagger stick, which he twirled and spun in a fashion that indicated hours of practice.

The major blathered on for many minutes, taking credit for the soldiers' accomplishments while managing to toady up to Colonel Anderson, who stood by with a forced patience, barely concealed. Tucker clenched his teeth to prevent any expression. Eyes straight ahead, he noticed the colonel's muddy boots, wrinkled fatigues, and crusher-style wool hat with a dull leather brim.

The major ended his prolonged remarks and stepped aside for the colonel, who regarded the men carefully. Tucker's shoulders squared themselves as if working on their own, chin rising slightly to offer the illusion of tallness. The colonel's head was lipless and long-necked, his back straight as a fence post. His sloped shoulders hunched forward as if his face led the rest of his body. Three deep lines furrowed both sides of his face, with shorter creases hooking around his mouth, linked by many other lines like the dried remains of tributaries. He wore a small gray mustache. He stood stalwart as stone, then walked with the fluidity of a creek. Tucker couldn't figure where on God's green earth the colonel had upped from. He seemed young and old simultaneously, the same way a newborn resembled his great-grandpa.

Colonel Anderson spoke in a soft tone, almost mild, but he clipped each word at its end, enabling his voice to reach all the soldiers. He offered the men an opportunity to join a special operations group. They'd work behind enemy lines against the Chinese who were reinforcing North Korean troops. The training included basic medical care, sabotage, explosives, hand-to-hand combat techniques, evasion, and orienteering. Operations would be vital, difficult, and dangerous.

"Your job," he said matter-of-factly, "is to jump out of airplanes and kill the enemy. I'm looking for volunteers."

Tucker raised his hand immediately. Behind him came the swift rustle of cloth as other men lifted their arms. The colonel scanned the formation, his face expressionless. The sun rose behind him, throwing his long shadow across the dirt. Tucker slitted his eyes against the glare. He'd never been in a plane, had never seen one except from a distance on the base airfield.

Major Buckner's head intensified its hue from pink to red to crimson as if sustaining a sunburn's full effects in a few seconds. His upper lip lifted in contempt as he saw seven men still with their arms down.

"When the colonel asks for volunteers," he said, "you damn well volunteer."

An insect veered from the sky and he swatted at it without contact. Red flesh bulged around the chin strap of his hat. He pointed at a large man beside Tucker, blonde-haired from Minnesota, the ghost of his Viking ancestry coursing through his veins.

"You." The major's voice became shrill with indignation. "Why didn't you raise your hand?"

The man blinked rapidly, his pale eyelashes fluttering. Outraged, the major lifted his swagger stick and struck the big man's leg a sharp blow that echoed across the drill yard. The soldier grimaced and stared straight ahead. Buckner hit the man twice more, the sound loud as an ax chop. The major turned to Tucker.

"What's your fucking buddy's fucking problem?"

"I don't know, sir," Tucker said.

"Find out."

Rivulets of sweat flowed down Swede's ruddy face. He could run all day with a full ruck, carrying the heavy BAR, and never complain. He was shy due to a speech impediment, compounded by a fourth-grade education. Swede took everything literally.

"Tell me," Tucker said to him. "Or he'll beat on us both."

"Pa-a-toot," Swede said.

"Parachute, sir," Tucker said to Major Buckner.

"What? Speak up."

"The colonel," Tucker said, "he didn't say nothing about a parachute."

The major lifted his swagger stick but Colonel Anderson was tired of the preening martinet. "Stop," he ordered, his voice edged with hardness.

Major Buckner stiffened, slowly bringing his stick to parade rest, tucked tightly beneath his left arm, parallel to the hard ground. He took two steps backward and returned to the colonel.

"Sir," the major said, "these men are a disgrace. They will be disciplined severely."

The colonel ignored him. "Volunteers stay," he said, and pointed at the big man from Minnesota. "You stay."

"Ten hut," the major said, watching in smug satisfaction as the soldiers saluted in unison. "Cowards dismissed."

Colonel Anderson waited until the six soldiers were out of sight before speaking. "Give me your stick."

The major presented his burnished swagger stick with a slight flourish. Colonel Anderson lifted his leg and snapped the stick across his knee. He dropped the splintered sections to the earth.

"Never hit a soldier in my army," he said. "Dismissed, Major."

Face blanched and eyes wide, the major saluted with an uncontrollable tremor to his hand. He pivoted and marched away, his gait slightly off-kilter as if the lack of his beloved instrument affected his balance.

Colonel Anderson approached the big Minnesotan.

"What's your name, soldier?"

"Lund."

"Do they call you 'Swede'?"

Lund nodded, perplexed that the colonel was so prescient.

"Would it make a difference if you received paratrooper training?"

"Uh . . ."

"Would you jump out of a plane if I gave you a parachute?"

Lund frowned briefly, then his face relaxed with comprehension. He raised his hand, nodding his head.

"How's your leg?" the colonel said.

Lund shrugged. Colonel Anderson circled the formation, now ragged with holes from missing men. He faced the miniature soldier in the center who'd spoken, smooth-faced and short, like a child wearing fatigues. His arm was still high, fingers extended to the sky.

"How tall are you?" the colonel said.

"Five foot five and one-quarter, sir," Tucker said.

"You positive about that one-quarter?"

"Yes, sir."

"You full grown?"

"I don't know, sir. I hope not."

The colonel nodded as if turning over the answer in his mind while concealing his amusement.

"Why'd you join my army, soldier?" the colonel said.

"To get away from home, sir."

"Where's home?"

"Just this side of the Rowan County line, here in Kentucky."

"You didn't get very far."

"No, sir. But there's more sky here."

"Is that why you volunteered for Airborne?"

"No, sir."

"Tell me why, son."

"I like birds."

The colonel nodded. Kids, he thought. Three years into war and he was left with kids. The advent of Chinese reinforcements for North Korea had resulted in a stalemate on the ground. The United States was not taking advantage of its air superiority. The Americans had made only two drops, both large scale and both successful, but afterward the paratroopers were used as infantry. The colonel believed that helicopters could drop small independent forces into carefully chosen regions. It had required a great deal of politicking on his part to arrange for the creation of a small, specialized force of paratroopers. The boys standing before him represented his first effort at assembling a ferocious new force.

Tucker and the other men trained for eight weeks, then began fast-moving operations in Korea. They fought and advanced, fought and advanced. Each action proved successful, despite severe losses. Within four months Tucker was combat-hardened and promoted in rank. He'd jumped twenty-four times and shot many enemy. Other men kept track of their kills, the same ones who bragged about the number of whores they'd had on leave. Tucker avoided those men. He maintained his weapons and his health. Everything about army life bored him except battle. Then the war ended.

He was shipped to a San Diego port, and put on a train going east. Military men were on every car, mostly wearing some version of their uniforms, eager to discuss their plans, their hometowns, and their women. They drank and fought in the club car. The passenger seats stank like drains. Tucker reached the end of his tolerance at Cincinnati's Union Station. He left the train and began walking home. He figured it was about a hundred miles, shorter if he avoided roads and traveled overland. If he got tired, he'd use part of his army pay to buy a horse.

Now, Tucker awoke hungry in Kentucky, momentarily bewildered, believing that the hills and heavy woods were the vestige of a dream and he was still in Korea. He lit a cigarette and relaxed in the familiar landscape. Swede was dead. Two-thirds of the men he knew were dead. Tucker attributed his own survival to a combination of luck and cunning. He shot quicker. In hand-to-hand combat, he struck first.

The morning woods reverberated with the droning hum of locusts, rising and falling as if they were a chorus led by a master insect. They stopped abruptly. The silence lasted half a minute, then they began again, confounding him with their ability, like a flock of birds changing direction as a group. He ate a piece of dried meat, sipped from his canteen, and began walking. After half a mile he cut a section of morning glory vine and used it to tie the Ka-Bar knife scabbard to his thigh. Freeman's pistol was snugged neatly into his belt, covered by his shirttail.

The dogwoods had already lost their blossoms, but the redbud still hazed the lower tree line. He avoided roads, traversing the open fields of dogbane and burdock. The occasional fence alerted him to the possibility of people. He followed a deer trail, wishing for a rifle. He kept himself aimed southeast, and came upon a dirt lane that led to a road covered with creek rock. His supplies had dwindled but he'd be all right. Anybody who couldn't live in the woods shouldn't be drawing breath.

At midday he rested in the cool shade of a copse of oak. He held the pistol in his lap and listened for the rattle of branches overhead. A tree limb dipped as a squirrel leaped from an adjacent oak. Tucker aimed at the gap where the tree trunk made its first split. He pursed his lips and made a short whirring noise. The squirrel's head rose in the oak's crotch, curious about the foreign sound. Tucker shot and the animal vanished in a brief crimson spray. He retrieved the squirrel and left the woods for an open field, picking henbit and dandelion. He hunted for the folded leaves of wood sorrel, and dug fourteen of the tuberous roots. A cluster of wild ramps drew him by their heavy garlicky scent. He took several plants.

Three hours later he encountered a tight run of barbed wire that held a piece of hide torn from a cow. He crossed the fence, alert to a possible bull, and followed the winding depression left by hooves, figuring the path led to a pond fed by a spring. At the source, he filled his canteen and washed the wood sorrel bulbs and wild greens.

The afternoon sun eased toward the horizon in ragged strips of scarlet. He left the pasture for the woods. A whip-poor-will's mournful call slid through the trees. On a rise in the land he found a limestone outcrop suitable to bivouac. Twin ruts of an old dirt road ran nearby, the middle rounded by high weeds, and he figured the road was used in fall for deer hunting. The cliff offered a commanding view of a field with a few trees and high grasses.

He dumped his ruck and rested. Dusk was coming on. The squirrel wasn't autumn-plump, but it had gained a little spring weight. He skinned and gutted it, then rinsed the carcass with canteen water, wishing he had his helmet to cook in. He fed hardwood sticks to the fire, a few at a time, while slicing the wood sorrel roots, using a flat rock for a cutting board. When the blade dulled, he sharpened it on the rock, an expedience he admired—the surface that dulled it could refresh it as well.

Darkness arrived gradually, then in a rush, shutting the space between the trees, dulling the limestone's sheen, draping the field below. He skewered the squirrel carcass on the green stick and cooked it slowly. The moon rose. He placed the ramps beside the fire, turning them several times. After thirty minutes he ate the best meal he'd had in a year.

The night air cooled quickly. He extinguished the fire with dirt, lit a Lucky, and reclined. Maybe he'd stay here a couple of days. Home wasn't going anywhere, and wasn't all that much anyhow—two hundred people in the woods, their houses linked by dirt roads and paths along the ridgelines. He knew everyone who lived there. A barred owl called and he listened for the higher-pitched squawking of a female but none answered. The owl was as alone as he was. He smoked the cigarette to the nub and saved it for later. He closed his eyes and slept.

Chapter Three

The sound of morning birds awoke Tucker early and he lay watching the sky change from indigo to pink to sheer light. He spent most of the day scouting his location. It was a good spot, safe and away from people, sheltered on high ground against rain. He could trap rabbits with a simple snare. He'd never eaten acorns but knew people had during the Depression. Families had fared better in the hills than elsewhere—they were already accustomed to living without much money and relying on the woods to get by.

Tucker filled his canteen at the creek and searched the bank until he found a turtle shell, bleached from the sun, the exterior panels of color having peeled away long ago. He slipped it in his ruck. He circled a limestone outcrop facing west, moving slowly and watching the brown rock mottled by sun. Late in the day he saw his prey—a heavy-bodied timber rattlesnake basking in the sun, docile as if it had recently come out of hibernation. Tucker counted eight rattles, which meant a young snake, maybe three years old.

Tucker withdrew his knife. He moved carefully, staying in the shade to prevent his shadow from falling over the snake. In a sudden motion, he stomped his boot just behind the snake's head and chopped its head off. Tucker leaped back, watching the severed head. It twisted on the rock, opening and closing its jaws, still fighting in a way he admired. For a full five minutes the body coiled and uncoiled, the rattles clicking in the air.

He carried the snake's body to his camp, skinned it, and cleaned it. He built a fire, poured water into the turtle shell, boiled the milkweed shoots, then added snake meat. After eating he sprawled on the ground, admiring the night sky and smoking a Lucky.

In the morning, Tucker ate the last of the snake and went to the creek to refill his canteen and wash the turtle shell. After walking a series of concentric circles in a mile radius, he was satisfied by the lack of human sign. He removed his clothes and bathed in a pool. The clear water magnified sight, making the smooth flat rocks that lined the bottom appear large and close. Crawdads scuttled backward, tiny claws poised in defense. He used sandstone as a crude sponge to scrub his skin red. His feet were still marked by combat boots like the scar on a tree where barbed wire had been nailed for years. He relaxed, letting the fresh water wash away the days of filth.

Tucker dressed in the sun and headed back to camp. Late-morning light spread overhead, sifting through the trees like golden liquid. He stopped moving in mid-stride.

Something was off-kilter. He listened intently, twitching his head in different directions, sniffing the air. His body calmed itself, a trait developed in combat. He became utterly still. His intuition had kept him alive in Korea and he'd learned to obey it, letting a kind of hidden awareness of the world govern his actions. He saw nothing, smelled nothing, and heard nothing. Abruptly he knew what was wrong—the lack of sound. The birds had ceased.

He moved upslope and climbed a low maple. Parked on the road two hundred yards away was a Chevrolet two-door Fleetmaster, black and shiny in the sun. Tucker eased down the tree and walked on the downwind side of the road. He needed to break camp before discovery. He heard the car's engine and rolled into a blackberry thicket beside the road. Thorns stabbed his face and arms. Bees lifted momentarily, then returned, and he sustained six stings but remained silent.

A young woman in a dark blue dress ran along the road as if fleeing the car behind her. The rocky road slowed her pace. A silver ribbon in her hair bobbed behind her as she ran. The Chevy overtook her easily, the driver yelling. She ran faster but the car swerved around her, bouncing over the uneven ground, and stopped sideways in the road. The driver emerged, a freshly shaved man in his thirties wearing a tight suit, hair slicked back with grease. He moved toward her and she slapped him twice, the second time hooking her fingers into claws. The man grabbed her hair, yanked her backward, and pushed her onto her hands and knees. With his free hand he grasped the hem of her dress and jerked it. The fabric tore, and half the dress slid off her body.

Tucker wriggled out of the briars and walked along the road. He had no plan but didn't like what he saw. The man was trying to tug her underpants down. His face was bleeding from her fingernails. She was silent, fighting him with no tears or wasted breath. Her underpants ripped, and the man tore them off. Tucker approached him from behind. The man was tall and broad shouldered with long arms, and weighed a good fifty pounds more than Tucker.

"Hey," Tucker said. "Having fun?"

The man stood upright, still clutching the woman's hair. He'd gotten a good grip by wrapping it around his fist and holding it at the base of her skull. Tucker had startled him but the man realized he was just a kid.

"Hell, yes," the man said.

"Best turn loose of her hair, then."

"Don't reckon I will, boy. You go on and get before I take that knife off your belt, stick it up your ass, and break the handle off."

The man smirked and spat, and gave the woman's hair a quick tug. Her head jerked but she didn't make a sound, just stared at Tucker with eyes as dark as walnut hulls. Tucker casually withdrew his pistol and aimed it at the man.

"Let her go," Tucker said.

The man didn't like the situation. In ten seconds it had gone from the best day in years to among the worst. He grinned, pulled the woman to her feet, and stood behind her. She kicked him in the shin with her heels. He lifted his knee hard between her legs, the force raising her off the ground. She gasped and her mouth fell open and Tucker saw how tiny her body was.

"You going to shoot me?" the man said.

"No."

"Didn't think so."

"Ain't got but three bullets," Tucker said. "Need them for squirrels."

The man laughed. He put his free hand around the woman's throat and started moving backward to the car.

"You're an honest fucker," the man said. "I give you that. But if you ain't shooting, I ain't waiting."

Tucker walked toward the man. The woman was breathing hard, her eyes sharp on him. Tucker set the pistol and knife on the ground, opened his hands to show them empty, and moved closer.

"Just fists?" the man said. "Or fists and boots?"

"However you want it. I might use a rock."

The man laughed and lifted his fists. Tucker struck him three times in the head, his arm moving like a piston in a quick flurry. The man staggered backward, and the woman ran to the car. The man lifted his arms to defend himself, then kicked Tucker in the knee. Pain flared along his leg, numbing it momentarily, and he thought he might fall. The man swung a wide looping right that Tucker ducked easily. He hopped to one side, favoring the hurt leg, and the man smiled lazily, a fearsome sight. Tucker had never seen a man who liked to grin and fight. Blood stained his teeth.

"Come on, runt," the man said. "I'll knock the taste out of your mouth."

Tucker picked up a rock, feinted left, and clubbed the man twice in the face. The first blow staggered him, gashing the skin to the bone above his eye. The second one hit his mouth, knocking two teeth out and driving him to his knees. A long thread of blood arced into the dirt.

"Stop," the woman said.

Tucker looked at her, waiting, his hand poised to strike.

"He's family," she said.

He lowered his arm, appreciating her loyalty, surprised at his own willingness to heed. She hurtled past him and kicked the man in the groin. His head tipped back and he fell in the dirt and vomited. Tucker retrieved his weapons. She kicked him three more times, then sat on the running board to rest.

The man was semiconscious, bleeding fiercely from a deep cut through his eyebrow, one tooth showing through his bottom lip. The blood was already drawing flies that shifted their focus to the more alluring pool of bile. Tucker avoided looking at the half-clothed woman. She'd had enough bad luck for one day and he didn't figure to add to it. He limped up the hill to his camp and packed his supplies. He sat and bent his leg a few times until satisfied that his knee was good enough to walk.

The woman stepped into view, having followed him up the hill. She'd torn a strip of fabric from the dress and used it to make a ragged sash that encircled her body for the sake of civility. Red finger marks emblazoned her neck. Her knees were scraped and bloody.

"You living up here?" she said.

"I'm leaving."

She noticed the dried snake hide curling on the ground, bits of blood and meat covered with dirt.

"Been eating on snake?" she said.

"I'd offer you some but it's gone."

"Not hungry."

He gave her the canteen and she drank deeply.

"I love water," she said.

"I'd say that's handy."

She wiped her mouth with the back of her hand and looked at his makeshift camp carefully.

"Are you on the run?" she said.

"Not till now, I don't reckon."

"This is my family's land you're on."

"I'll get on out of here, then."

"I didn't mean it that way," she said. "Just that I know all my kin and neighbors and I ain't never laid eyes on you."

"I was in the army. I'm going home now. War's over."

"Where at?"

"Korea."

"No, I mean where's home?"

Her skin was brown, her black hair glossy and thick. Her cheekbones were as prominent as railroad gravel. She was as small a woman as he'd ever seen.

"You mind if I smoke a Lucky?" he said. "Then I'll go on and go."

She shook her head. He sparked a smoke and squatted. His little dream of laying up here for the summer had evaporated as fast as morning fog. He would refill the canteen, then head east, figuring he could make ten miles before dark.

"Should've said this already," she said. "But thank you."

He nodded and looked away.

"Who is that feller?" he said.

"My uncle."

"Why are you dressed up?"

"Funeral," she said. "My daddy's. It was this morning. Uncle Boot said he'd give me a ride home. I shouldn't a took it. But I did."

"Say your daddy died?"

"A horse threw him. He landed bad and been sick two months."

"Reckon your mom's pretty tore up about it."

"She was till they buried him. Then she perked right up and wanted a drink. That's part of why I took a ride off Uncle Boot."

"He your dad's brother or your mom's?"

"Mom's. She'll side with him. She always did. The sun, it rises and sets on him. It's sure going to set on him today. I can't go back to that house no more."

"How old are you?" he said.

"Going on fifteen. How old are you?"

"What's today?"

"Saturday."

"I mean what day of the month."

"The date?" she said.

"Uh-huh."

"The twentieth."

"Are we still yet in May?"

"That's right."

"I'll be eighteen in ten days."

"You don't look it," she said.

"Your uncle didn't think so either. Reckon I ort to check on him, seeing as how he's your kin."

He stood, testing his injured knee.

"Your leg hurt?" she said.

"Not bad," he said. "It's the bee stings aggravating me."

"I can make a salve."

"Maybe in a minute."

He stepped past her and walked down the slope. Uncle Boot was leaning against a tire, breathing hard and ragged through his mouth. Blood covered the left side of his face, still running in stripes along his jaw and dripping onto his shirt. At Tucker's approach, he cupped the front of his pants with one hand.

"Didn't have to kick me in the nuts," Uncle Boot said.

"I never," Tucker said. "That was your niece done that."

"Rhonda?"

"All I did was hit you a few times."

The man wiped blood from his face.

"Is it pretty bad?"

"No," Tucker said. "A cut to the head bleeds a lot." He bent down and inspected the man's wound. "Ain't too deep. Can you see out of both eyes?"

"I don't know. I ain't tried to yet."

Tucker picked up a scrap of torn dress and held it to the man's face, blotting the blood.

"Now open that eye," he said.

The man blinked several times. He closed the other eye, then nodded. Tucker was glad he hadn't blinded him. The girl stepped past Tucker and kicked him in the groin again. Drool dribbled down Uncle Boot's chin. Tucker shook his head at her.

"You done enough," he said. "Don't mess with him no more."

"Who the hell are you?" Uncle Boot said.

"Nobody," Tucker said. "I'm heading up to Ohio to see my wife."

Rhonda clamped her lips together hard as stacked rock. Tucker knew he should walk away, not say another word, just set off walking and let them think he was headed north.

"Will you run me home?" The man's voice was gaspy at the edges. "I ain't sure I can drive. Swelled up down there like a couple of gourds."

"Run you home?" Tucker said.

"I'll pay you if you want."

Rhonda was at the mercy of two men and hated them both for it, but mainly hated herself for being in the situation—one she'd created by getting in the car with her uncle. She knew what he'd had in mind. She'd known it for years, but didn't figure he'd try anything the day of the funeral. She was getting angrier by the second. Mainly she was mad at the soldier for being married.

"All right," Tucker said. "You lay down in the backseat. She's going to watch you from the front. You move one finger, and I'll turn her loose on you again."

"You going to give her the gun?" Uncle Boot said.

"No, I ain't."

"That's a damn blessing," Uncle Boot said.

Tucker opened the car door and pushed the seat forward to make space for Uncle Boot. He wondered how far away Uncle Boot lived. Rhonda's underpants lay in the road like the flag of a fallen country and he tried not to think about her legs under the remnants of her dress. They'd looked strong when she kicked, thigh muscles hard as cordwood.

Uncle Boot realized he'd get no assistance and began moving carefully, a few inches at a time, crawling like a baby up the running board, and into the backseat. He lay there panting, testicles aching, nausea spreading in waves.

Tucker threw his ruck in the middle of the bench seat and inserted himself behind the wheel with the pistol in his lap. Rhonda stood in the road.

"Come on," Tucker said. "I can't carry him and leave you."

"Last time I got in that car was a mistake."

"I reckon it was."

Tucker depressed the clutch, pumped the accelerator twice, and turned the key. The Chevy caught, backfired, and began idling with enough power to quiver the car. He shifted into reverse, backed in a half circle, then maneuvered toward the main road. He looked at Rhonda through the passenger window. Finally, he leaned across his ruck and opened the door.

"Stubborn's good," he said. "But ain't no sense in being foolish right now."

"I ain't the fool here."

"You're right. I didn't mean it that way."

He gave the car a little gas, watching her face for a trace of fear. None came. She was stoic as a block of granite. A breeze rustled her hair, flinging a strand across her face. She ignored it.

"I won't lay a hand on you," Tucker said. "Give you my word."

He nodded once, a quick lowering of the chin to indicate his sincerity. She got in the car and he drove across the ground, flushing a partridge from a clump of tall grass. She sat with her back to the door, watching her uncle in the backseat, smirking at his occasional moan. Tucker figured his pain wasn't that bad, he just didn't want to get hurt again. At a T-intersection of dirt roads Tucker stopped for instructions.

"Left," Rhonda said.

The car handled extremely well, the best Tucker had ever driven, much better than army vehicles. It was heavy enough not to slide in loose rock, and the shocks were strong as he bounced through potholes. Rain running off the hillside had left a series of gullies in the road like giant corduroy, jarring the car. Rhonda directed him onto the blacktop then a country lane, and finally onto a dirt road that followed a creek between two hills.

"Slow down up here," she said.

Tucker rounded a sharp curve and braked. The road dipped down a muddy bank into a slow-moving creek. The water was clear enough to see a set of car tracks on the bottom.

"Bridge warshed out," Rhonda said.

"I don't know if this rig will make it," Tucker said. "I'd hate to get stuck."

"Uncle Boot drove through it this morning."

"This your place?"

"Yeah," she said.

The house had a low roof that sloped to a narrow porch. Car tires held shingles in place against the wind that he knew came flying down the holler, trapped between the hills. Snugged into a cluster of honeysuckle was an outhouse constructed of green wood. The lumber had warped with time until the shack leaned sideways with wide cracks between the boards.

"You'uns need you a new outhouse," he said.

"I know it," she said. "It's full of waspers, too."

"Who's home?" he said. "And how many live here?"

"Nobody. Mommy went to my sister's. I was supposed to meet them there."

"Where's your uncle live at?"

"Here," she said quietly. "He's been staying here since Daddy got sick."

Tucker eased the big car into the creek. The rear end dropped and he gave it a little gas, yanking the wheel to find traction, moving forward quickly, jumping the opposite bank. He hit the brakes hard and cut the tires to avoid the flat slabs of creek rock that formed the porch foundation.

"Go get your stuff," he said.

"My stuff?"

"I ain't leaving you here with this bucket-head."

She hurried into the house. Tucker got out of the car and dragged Uncle Boot into the yard. His face was swollen. The caked blood cracked like mud and peeled away. He spat a tooth. The day hadn't turned out the way he'd planned, just when he was about to finally tear a piece off Rhonda. He'd been smart, he'd bided his time, he'd taken care of his sister's dying husband. Now a boy with odd eyes had beat him down to the ground and half into it.

Tucker pulled Uncle Boot across the muddy grass to three board steps that led to the porch. He moaned and reached for the front of his pants, then moaned louder. Tucker went to the car for his ruck, retrieved the moonshine, shook the jar vigorously, and examined the bubbles. The bead rode the surface of the liquid a little high. At least it wasn't below the surface, a much worse sign. He opened the glove box and dug out the car's title of ownership.

He returned to Uncle Boot and held one hand behind his neck, cradling his head, and offered a sip of liquor. The harsh smell served to wake him slightly and he tried to jerk his head away, but when he understood what was in the jar, he relaxed and drank. The moonshine burned several wounds in his mouth. He drank again and leaned back.

Tucker held the pink slip in front of Uncle Boot's good eye.

"I aim to buy your car," Tucker said.

"Ain't for sale."

"I'll give you two hundred dollars."

"You shit and fall back in it."

"I'll put the sheriff on your ass," Tucker said. "You tried to mess with your niece who ain't but fourteen. They'll throw you in the pokey."

Uncle Boot laughed, a rough sound that shifted to a hoarse cough. He spat blood.

"Son," he said. "I am the goddam sheriff."

Tucker rocked back on his heels, squatting, elbows propped on his knees, arms extended in front of him. It was his pondering pose and he needed to think his way out of a mess he shouldn't be in. Two hours ago he'd been lying happily in a creek. A sense of longing for the army passed through him—explicit instructions had simplified life. Now he had to think like an officer and issue orders to himself.

The screen door creaked and banged, hinged on strips of rubber cut from an old tire. A panel of cardboard patched the rusting screen. Rhonda came onto the porch holding two bulging pillowcases and a basket covered with a quilt.

"He really the sheriff?" Tucker said.

"Deputy," she said.

"No," Uncle Boot said. "Sheriff's out of the county. I'm the law for three more days."

"Where's your gun at?" Tucker said.

"In the house. Didn't think it was right taking it to the funeral."

"You got ary a phone?" Tucker said to Rhonda.

She shook her head.

"Neighbors got one?"

"No," she said. "We use my sister's, about four miles away. Her husband is a truck driver so they have one."

Tucker nodded as if that made any sense. All that mattered was Uncle Boot not calling anybody.

"I aim to have you sign this car to me," Tucker said. "Two hundred cash money. Or everybody up and down this holler will know you got your ass whipped by me, not even eighteen years old. You won't do much lawing after that."

Rhonda stepped around Uncle Boot and began loading her possessions into the car.

"Get me a ink pen," Tucker said to her. "And bring his gun out here."

She nodded and went back into the house. He could hear drawers opening and slamming shut. Tucker leaned his face close to Uncle Boot. He slid the Ka-Bar out and pressed the edge to the man's neck.

"One night you'll be asleep and hear something and think maybe it's a raccoon but it ain't. It'll be me. And I'll rip you like a fish. You hear me. Don't think I won't. Only reason you ain't dead is being her kin."

Uncle Boot's good eye widened. He could feel the blade against his carotid artery and worried that if his heart started pumping too fast, the vein might puff out and he'd wind up cutting his own throat. The boy was crazy as a rat in a coffee can. Uncle Boot was tired of the car anyway. He'd confiscated it from a shine runner and didn't care for the way it handled without the heavy weight, like a dump truck with no load. The former owner was in a federal prison and not likely to come hunting his rig for years.

"Three hundred," Uncle Boot said.

"Two hundred," Tucker said. "And I'll throw in the liquor."

Rhonda stepped onto the porch with a thirty-eight pistol and a ballpoint pen that advertised a funeral home. Tucker sheathed the knife. He spread the title out on the oak step, worn smooth from years of shoe leather, and began methodically pulling folded sheaves of money from his pockets. Rhonda stared, entranced as if witnessing a magic trick—the man's clothes were made of money. He counted the bills into a pile, and Uncle Boot signed the title. Tucker took the pistol from

Rhonda, removed the bullets, and threw them in the creek. He tossed the gun onto the porch roof.

Tucker hauled Uncle Boot to his feet and walked him through the dim front room and deposited him on the couch. Uncle Boot nodded thanks but Tucker ignored him. He wasn't doing the man a favor. He didn't want anybody driving by to see a bloody man lying on the steps.

Outside, Rhonda stood still and silent as a tree. He didn't know if she was waiting on him or afraid of him.

"What county is this?" he said.

"Fleming. Why?"

"So I know to stay out of it."

Tucker went to the car and started it. Rhonda joined him and he made a three-point reverse turn and crossed the creek. She sat primly in the front seat, staring through the windshield. She'd changed clothes and pinned her hair up. In her lap was a small box her father had made of cedar, the dovetailed pins and tails interlocking as tight as the day he'd finished.

Tucker focused on the road, glancing at the mirror for signs of pursuit. The gas gauge indicated enough fuel to get out of the county before nightfall. He had two hundred forty dollars left, plenty of money. He tried to light a Lucky but the flame blew out. He tried again. Rhonda took the cigarette and lighter and got it going and passed it back to him. Their eyes met briefly and both looked away at the same time.

"Where do you want me to take you?" he said.

"I ain't a-caring."

"Sister's house? Town? Where at?"

"Where you're going for now," she said. "Is that all right?"

Tucker nodded and drove. Rhonda's insides tingled like a bottle of shook-up pop. She'd wanted out of that house and holler for years but wasn't about to do what her sisters had done—marry the first boy who came around by making sure to get pregnant. No, she'd have none of that.

A part of her wished Uncle Boot wasn't her uncle so Tucker could have gone ahead and killed him. She'd wanted to ever since he started brushing up against her accidental-like in the house, then jumping back as if it was her fault. She'd never told anyone because no one would believe her, and she'd slept with an ice pick under her pillow. Now she was out, she was free. She pulled the bobby pins loose and clipped them to her collar for safekeeping. She leaned her head out the window, squinting against the wind. Her hair flowed like liquid in the air. She'd never felt as good in her life.

Chapter Four

Tucker drove on back roads, leaving Fleming County and crossing a wooden bridge over the Licking River into his home county. He didn't talk, just drove. Mainly he was trying to ignore Rhonda's satiny brown legs. All the women in his family were blond-headed with blue eyes, heavy-hipped, and tall. Rhonda's dark eyes had brows that lay along her face like embroidery. The best he could do was not look at her at all.

He left the bridge for the blacktop and parked in a wide spot strewn with fishermen's litter—knotted line, lost lures, and a broken crawdad trap. He got out of the car and stretched his legs. The river was high from spring rain, debris distributed from a surge that he figured had come last week, judging by the amount of dirt encasing the driftwood. He scratched his bee stings. He walked to the water's edge and admired a turtle sunning itself on a fallen maple, its roots eroded away. He wondered why a tree grew so close to the same water that would make it fall. Maybe trees were as greedy as people.

He climbed the slope to the road and checked the radiator, which was full, no leaks. The oil level was good and the tires held air. He knew Rhonda was watching him but he refused to meet her eyes.

"You want to know something?" she said.

He shrugged.

"The Licking River is the longest in the world," she said.

"I don't know about that."

"It's all the turns and twists. You was to straighten it out, just grab hold of it and shake it like a rope, it'd be longer than any of them."

He looked at the river, gauging the veracity of her words, trying to figure out how anybody could grab a river.

"You don't believe me, do you," she said.

"I don't know what to believe."

"It's the truth. I read it in a book."

"A book."

"Yep," she said. "I like to read. You?"

"I ain't had much luck with that."

He used his shirtsleeve to brush a skim of dust from the outside mirrors. Not many cars had them on both sides and he examined the passenger mirror. Two new screws held it in place and he wondered why someone had bolted it on.

He opened the canteen and offered it to Rhonda, keeping his eyes downcast until seeing her slim ankles, then jerked his head as if struck by a rock. She tipped her head and drank, her throat moving like a hummingbird. She lowered the canteen and caught him looking.

"What?" she said.

He opened the door and got in. The upholstering already felt molded to his body and the pedals had just enough give. He waited for her but she stayed in the road and after ten minutes he left the car and asked her what was wrong.

"Where are we going?" she said.

"I don't know exactly. I was aiming for home but I can't just show up with you."

"Why not? Something wrong with me?"

"That ain't it," he said. "My mom died. Afterward my sister got churched up. She'd not let you stay the night. Wouldn't be right."

"I'll sleep in the car."

"That'd be worse. You could stay with my other sister, but you'd not like her."

"How do you know?"

"Nobody does, not even her husband and kids."

"How come?"

"She's like a blue jay. Pretty to look at but loud and mean."

She laughed, the sudden sound so full of genuine merriment that Tucker felt momentarily discombobulated. She had a broad smile that showed just enough pink gum to make her look like a little kid, accentuated by the tip of her tongue sticking out between her teeth. A small dark bug was on the right side of her face.

"Watch that," he said, and brushed his own cheek. "Think it's a tick."

She wiped her jaw.

"Did I get it?" she said.

"No."

She wiped harder, lifting her eyebrows to him, and he shook his head. She leaned toward him, cocking her jaw.

"Get it off me," she said. "I despise a tick."

He lifted his hand and stopped as he realized it was a mole.

"Uh . . ." he said. "It ain't nothing."

She laughed again.

"It's my beauty mark," she said. "Movie stars in magazines got them, too."

He walked to the other side of the car and fumbled for a Lucky. He should never have started looking at her, let alone talking. A large cloud moved across the sky, crumbling into tattered shards that bunched up like a herd of sheep. He heard the rapid cry of a rain crow and looked in the weeds for its long bill aimed toward the sky.

"Hear that?" he said.

She nodded.

"Storm's coming," he said.

"I guess that bird told you that just now?"

He studied the earth for the dry residue of working ants until he found a series of their tiny mounds. The entrances were covered by dirt.

"See there," he said. "The ants are drawing up and closing their doors. A book ain't the only thing there is to read. We best get going if we're going to."

She walked to the car door but didn't open it. What now, he wondered.

"Why won't you look at me?" she said.

He glanced away.

"See there," she said. "Is it because your eyes being different colored? I don't care about that."

"That ain't it."

"Well, what then?"

He didn't answer.

"Tell me," she said, "or I ain't getting in that car again."

"I can't leave you here. And I can't take you back."

"Then why won't you look at me?"

He stared at the blacktop. Midday sun had heated the edge of the road enough to turn it soft. A blade of grass protruded from the imprint of a boot. He heard the rain crow again.

"On account," he said.

"Of what?"

"Of thinking you're pretty."

"What about that wife of yours up in Ohio?"

"I ain't got a wife," he said.

"So you lied."

"Not to you."

"If that was a lie, how do I know you ain't lying now."

"Don't reckon you do," he said. "I told your uncle that in case he chased after me. He'd go north hunting a married man."

He got back into the car and slammed the door and turned the key. The sky was dark in the west behind him, the air cooling rapidly, tree leaves tipped toward the ground. The storm was moving fast. Rhonda sat as far from him as possible. He nodded to himself, ratcheted the car into gear, and drove. It was a good thirty miles to his house, the last ten on dirt roads adjacent to creeks. The hollers were tight enough that mushrooms grew on both sides due to lack of light.

Four miles farther a ferocious wind hit the car and Tucker stopped on the side of the road. Hail drilled the roof. He peered through the windshield and saw lightning strike a beech. Two seconds later, the lightning shot from the earth, showering the car with chunks of dirt. Tucker realized that the lightning had traveled the length of the tree into the ground and along a root until it hit a rock and ricocheted back toward the sky. His chest felt light and he could smell a chemical scent. Rhonda scooted swiftly across the seat, reaching for him, pressing her head into his shoulder, arms clinging to his chest, her body trembling.

He'd never understood being afraid of a storm. It was just water. Half the planet was ocean and lake and river, and he'd heard that humans were mostly made of water, too. He believed that thunder occurred when two clouds bumped into each other. Lightning came from their friction, like sparks from scraped rocks, and rain was a kind of blood falling from the wounded clouds. He breathed evenly. The storm would pass and he didn't care one way or another.

Rhonda's shivering limbs and heartbeat thudding against his chest produced a series of unfamiliar sensations. He felt as if he was suddenly hungry for a kind of food he'd never known existed. He held her without moving. His arms and legs tingled as if shot through with a mild electrical pulse. He'd never felt so calm. He was rooting for the storm to stay, to increase intensity and prolong the new notion of himself—every cell cognizant of her.

Twigs and leaves pressed against the windshield before they were blown away by sudden gusts. The sky was black as night without the depth. The storm's center lingered overhead as if trapped between the hills, thunder echoing like artillery. A crack of lightning striking wood abruptly felled a tree across the road. He could smell the burned inner core of the trunk.

Rhonda clung tight as if trying to burrow into his body. Their breathing fogged the window and he smeared a porthole with his hand but there was nothing to see—the world was dark and wet and fierce. After an hour he dozed. Thunder woke him several times but the rain itself was soothing. At some point the storm began to move but night had arrived and the sky remained as dark as coal. Thunder faded to the pall of silence.

He woke at dawn, pressed against the car door, neck stiff, one arm gone dead from the weight of Rhonda's body. She was curled into herself on the broad bench seat, knees tucked high. She'd crooked an elbow beneath her head as a pillow but her other arm was around his waist, her fingers clutching his shirt. Occasionally her body twitched. Tucker tried to remain utterly still, aware of her warmth. He couldn't recall having slept with such proximity to any living body.

The sky became light gray overhead, but the woods beyond the automobile were a dark wall of trees. The sun lifted. He used his free hand to clean the condensation and saw a tree blocking the road—a poplar with bark seared from lightning. The sound of birds came tentatively at first, as if they didn't fully trust the weather, but as the sun imbued the land with golden light, the birds began in earnest.

Rhonda was lovely at rest, face relaxed, lips slightly parted. Hair surrounded her face like a black halo. He caressed her cheek gently, brushing aside stray strands of wispy hair. Her ear was tiny and snugged tight to her head. The back of her neck held a small furrow of muscle with a dark speck, another tiny mole. He sat without moving, marveling at her beauty. He feared that the roughness of his palm would disturb her and reversed his hand to stroke her face with the back of his fingers. Her cotton dress was thin enough that he could see the intricate structure of her collarbone, the small pocket in her shoulder surrounded by bone and cartilage. It was the ideal spot to place a four-leaf clover.

Despite his care, she stirred, shifting her slim body, stretching her legs until her feet touched the door. Her arm drifted from his waist, her hand settling against his leg. He gently moved her hand away and underwent a sense of relief. His experience with women was limited to one Korean hooker and even then, he'd been drunk but not drunk enough to fully engage. She'd touched him with her hand. He'd been grateful for the release, doubly grateful that he hadn't gone all the way since he wasn't married. He'd never told his buddies, knowing they'd jeer at him.

She breathed deeply and her eyelashes fluttered like the dainty wings of a butterfly. He watched her open her eyes, close them, open them again, and blink several times. She shifted, turning her body on the seat, looking up at him. Her eyes were soft and warm. She smiled, a small one as if testing the waters for something grander. He set his hand on the bottom of the steering wheel to protect her head in case she rose suddenly. With a dainty slowness, she slid her fingers between his. They looked at each other for a long time as the sun warmed the air. He wanted to speak but didn't know what to say and was afraid. She licked her lips.

"I love the light after a storm," she said. "The birds are always happier."

He nodded.

After a few minutes, she opened the car door and stepped out. His arm felt on fire as the blood rushed its length. He watched her go into the woods. He got out of the car and swung his arm around, feeling the sensation return to immobile fingers. He examined the poplar blocking the road. Strips of bark lay scattered among limbs and leaves. It was too heavy to move without a chainsaw. He searched the ground until finding a crescent of wood singed black by lightning.

Rhonda emerged from the woods, her ankles damp from dew. She hopped over a rain branch as nimbly as a yearling and came to him. He offered the piece of lucky wood. She smelled it and smiled at him, a full smile this time. She glanced at the poplar in the road that prevented their passage. She hadn't spent a single night away from family, and certainly never slept in an automobile. She'd only been in a car three times. The best part of her father's funeral had been riding in the backseat, dressed in her Sunday-go-to-meeting clothes, hoping to pass someone she knew.

The world appeared for the first time beautiful, the air scoured of dust by the rain, each leaf holding a sheen of water. She could smell the loam and wildflowers, hear the birds braiding their song along the land. In the purity of morning light she'd never seen anyone so handsome or strong as Tucker.

"What are we going to do?" she said.

"Get married, I reckon," he said. "We spent a night together already."

"I meant about this tree in the road."

"Back up to a wide place and turn around."

She nodded. What she saw as an obstacle, he regarded as just another thing to circumvent.

"You want to?" she said.

"Well, we can't stay here and wait for the tree to rot."

"No," she said. "I meant the other. What you said."

"Get married?"

She nodded.

"I meant it," he said. "I don't never say things I don't mean. You want to or not?"

Tucker matched her, she thought—small like her, serious and capable. She wondered if their children would have his eyes. She took his hand and silently vowed to stay near him forever. She would never forsake this man. They leaned together and gazed at the land. She hoped for a rainbow but none came and she understood that she was an adult now and adults didn't hope for what they couldn't control, but accepted what was there—the tree in the road, the woods, the soft thin blue of sky. The birds were already beginning to ease their song. She heard the swift rush of rain running to a creek. She stood on her tiptoes and touched her mouth to his ear.

"Yes," she whispered. "Yes, I do."

He thought about kissing her but decided he should wait. Unsure of protocol, he didn't want to make a mistake. He'd never seen anyone kiss before, and figured it was a habit for married people, best done in private.

The moon was in the sky, translucent as mist. Venus faded into the leaves of the trees. Yellow light glowed across the land. If Tucker had a chainsaw, he'd cut a car-sized gap in the downed poplar and head home. Instead he backed four miles along the road.

His neck began to ache from looking over his shoulder and he tried using the mirrors, glancing back and forth from the conventional mirror to the larger one bolted on the passenger side. He turned around at the fishing spot where they'd stopped the day before. Several times he had to drive off the edge of the road to avoid windblown limbs. The car handled in an impressive manner, heavy as a truck, the tires always grabbing tight. He became accustomed to the side mirrors and realized the extra one provided more visibility. He wondered if it was a rich man's vehicle.

Three hours later they arrived in town. Morehead sat in the widest holler in the hills, which allowed sufficient space for a train station, a hotel, three stores, and a diner. Tucker stopped at a filling station, where a man pumped gas into the car. He wore greasy coveralls with his name stitched in cursive on an oval patch: Chester.

Tucker went inside for a pack of smokes, two RC colas, a bag of peanuts, a Valomilk, and a moon pie. He had no idea what Rhonda might like and didn't want to go out and ask her in front of the gas station attendant. Chester came in, made change from a ten-dollar bill, and accompanied Tucker outside. He walked slowly around the car and gave a long low whistle of admiration.

"Nice rig," he said, then dropped his voice. "Who you running for?"

Tucker looked at him without talking.

"Don't tell me nothing," Chester said. "But I know a run-rig when I see it. If you got ary a spare jar, I don't mind a drink now and then."

"A run-rig."

"No need to play dumb. Fact is, I work on them. But I ain't seen this one before. If you ain't running for Beanpole,

I'd keep on going right straight out of the county. Beanpole ain't one to like competition."

"I just got out of the army," Tucker said. "Looking for work. Maybe I'll drive for Beanpole. How do I get hold of him?"

"You don't," Chester said. "A little bird will let him know and he'll get hold of you."

Tucker nodded.

"What's your name, buddy?" Chester said.

"Tucker. From the last hill on the line at Carter County."

"Say you're a Tucker? Heard you'uns was bad to be wild."

Tucker faced the man square on, shoulders relaxing on their own, breathing slowly. His fingers brushed the Ka-Bar hilt as he lifted his eyes to the man's face for the first time. Chester took a step back.

"Might not have been your bunch," Chester said. "Job like this, you hear a lot. Hard to keep the bullshit straight from the real."

"You tell Beanpole I'm real."

Tucker turned his back on the man, knowing Chester was all hole and no coal, a mouthy man pushing gas. In the car he gave Rhonda the pop and candy.

"How about we eat a regular meal at that diner yonder," she said. "I only ate in one once. They had the coldest Co-Colas ever was."

They sat in the back near the noisy kitchen, less for privacy than the sudden self-consciousness due to their bedraggled state. Eight other people ate lunch or drank coffee, all dressed better than Tucker and Rhonda. An older waitress brought them glasses of pop, french fries, and cheeseburgers. They ate quickly, then ordered milk shakes to go and walked to the car, eager to get away from the sidelong looks of town people. They didn't belong and everyone in there knew it, most of all Tucker and Rhonda.

They drove east along a dirt side road that ended at Triplett Creek. Tucker smoked while Rhonda finished her milk shake. For two hours they made plans. They'd get married in the Clay Creek Church of God and move into his great-grandfather's old house. He told her what Chester had said about Beanpole. She thought that if he had a run-car, he might as well put it to use. They'd need money for the kids they'd have. Tucker agreed with everything.

1964

Chapter Five

Hattie Johnson left Frankfort early, heading east toward the hills. She usually made the trip alone every three months, but this time her boss insisted on accompanying her. Hattie didn't like it. She worried that Marvin was finding fault or didn't trust her. He'd dismissed her concern, explaining that it was good for him to be in the field and get his hands dirty once in a while. Hattie didn't care for the implication that her job or the people she assisted were in any way dirty.

They entered the hills, thick and dense as if a bolt of heavy moleskin had been unfurled in a hurry, still bunched up, its folds and dips never straightened. Marvin opened a worn folder on his lap. It was labeled "Tucker," the ink slightly faded, thick with forms and reports. He thumbed through the file rapidly, then slowed and read it all, becoming more and more appalled.

"Are the parents related?" he said.

"No," she said. "First thing I checked."

"You sure?"

"Might be some overlap if you go far enough back, but not enough to worry over. I ran through state records and county."

"Any history in either one's family?"

"Nothing," she said.

"Water?"

"Tested out okay. Deep well, same as everybody thereabouts."

"We got to put a stop to it."

"No law against it," she said.

"There should be."

"Lots of things in families they can't help. I haven't seen a perfect one yet."

"This is a far cry from perfect," he said. "Why didn't you tell me?"

She stiffened slightly, fingers clenching the steering wheel. She cut him a quick glance but he wasn't being accusatory, just perplexed.

"I filed my reports," she said.

"I see that," he said. "For eight years, looks like. Who else knows?"

"Neighbors. Teachers. State doesn't send anyone but me."

"There has to be a reason."

"Bad luck, my opinion."

"Good gosh almighty," he said. "Does luck get this bad?"

"For some."

They drove through Morehead and followed the railroad tracks deeper into the hills. Walls of impenetrable forest covered the land. Marvin's anxiety grew as if he were entering a foreign country. The hills made him claustrophobic. Once in a while they passed a slight opening in the woods where a dirt lane led into a narrow gap. It was early autumn, still warm during the day, but Marvin shivered inside his clothes.

Past town, the blacktop became a series of dirt roads. Hattie stopped at the foot of a steep slope with a dry creek bed coming off the hill. She left the car and examined the dirt. Marvin joined her.

"What, pray tell, are you doing?" he said.

"Making sure we can pull the hill," she said. "Lot of clay in this land. Easy to get stuck if it's wet. But I don't think it's rained in a while. We can make it."

"Make it where?"

"Up the hill," she said and pointed to the creek bed. "That's the road."

"I need a minute," he said.

"You can wait here, if you want."

"No," he said. "I'll go, I'll go."

The air was silent save for the rumbling engine of her car. Hattie leaned on the rear fender. There were two Kentuckys, east and west, dirt and blacktop. She straddled them through her work. Marvin had made his first step across the boundary and was already out of sorts.

He inhaled as deeply as possible but the air didn't seem to reach the bottom part of his lungs. Everything felt thick and heavy—the air, the terrain, the woods. Maybe at the top of the hill he'd be able to breathe easier. He got in the car and shut the door carefully, preferring to keep all movement as slow as possible. Something existed in the hills he didn't want to disturb. It scared him and the fear made him angry. He wondered what kind of people lived here.

Hattie slid behind the wheel, battled the old clutch into low, and began climbing the hill, her feet moving among the pedals like playing a piano. Gravity pressed her against the seat. Tree limbs scraped the car on a sharp turn. The road flattened abruptly and a house presented itself in a wedge of trees. Scattered scraps of grass lay in patches on the bare earth. The small house had a new roof and a tar paper add-on tight against the hillside. A washtub covered the chimney to keep rain out.

Hattie honked twice, announcing her presence to the Tucker family. A scruffy brown dog lifted its lips to bare glinting teeth. A dirty yellow dog kept its distance. Marvin locked the car and Hattie grinned to herself. She'd never seen a dog yet that could operate a car door.

A young girl stepped onto the porch. She wore a homemade shift with no sleeves, its hand-sewn hems uneven and tattered. She slid two fingers into her mouth and whistled, then yelled. The yard dogs slank away, scruffs high like dorsal fins.

Hattie got out of the car and approached the house.

"Hidy, Jo," she said. "You all right?"

Jo nodded.

"Mommy's laying in the bed," she said.

"Well, all right," Hattie said. "I'll wait for her. Got something in the car you might like."

Jo's face didn't change, her expression maintaining its blank demeanor, freckled heavily as if by specks of flung gravy. She had thin arms and thin legs but Hattie wasn't worried—they were a small-framed bunch.

Marvin left the car, aware of his proximity to the dogs and the thick brush marking the edge of the hill. The road or driveway or creek bed—whatever they'd just traveled—ended at the house with no room to turn around, no way to flee quickly. He joined Hattie, determined to stay close. She opened the trunk. Snugged against the spare tire was a wooden milk crate containing a bar of chocolate and a small stuffed pony with a yellow mane and tail.

"Wouldn't a doll be a more appropriate gift?" Marvin said.

"Not really, no."

"All the kids like Betsy Braid, Dick Tracy's daughter."

"That girl doesn't need a doll to fool with," Hattie said. "You'll understand in a minute."

Jo skittered off the porch and across the yard, her tiny feet raising tufts of dust. Hattie handed her the chocolate.

"Thank ye," the girl said, her voice a shy muttering whisper.

She broke off a small piece, slid it in her mouth, and folded the paper around the rest. She smiled at Hattie, her dark eyes filled with appreciation. Hattie gave her the pony.

"It's a palomino," Hattie said. "You can name it yourself."

The girl examined the stuffed animal as if it were a foreign object discovered in a lost city.

"Store-bought, ain't it," she said.

"That's right," Hattie said. "It's from a factory in China."

"A factory horse," Jo said. "I'm going to name it China."

Hattie spoke quietly to Marvin's frown. "Most of the kids around here have homemade toys, but her mother hasn't been able."

Marvin nodded. The girl was slight as a vine, but appeared healthy and strong. Her limbs were well-muscled beneath her tan skin.

"How's the little ones?" Hattie said.

"Good," Jo said. "Same."

"And your mama?"

"She ain't much help here lately."

"Your daddy home?"

Jo shook her head, her tiny shoulders tensing slightly. Marvin decided it was time for him to exert authority.

"Is he working?" he said.

The little girl turned and ran to the porch, disturbing a chicken that had emerged from the woods and idly pecked at the yellow-clay dirt. Hattie leveled a stare at Marvin, flat as barn wood and twice as hard.

"What?" he said. "It's on the list of specific questions."

"More than one way to get answers," Hattie said. "Let me tell you something. You ask yes-or-no questions and you won't get anything. Folks around here don't think that way. A yes-or-no question will make them think there's a right answer and a wrong one. They won't speak because they don't want to make a mistake."

"How is being honest a mistake?"

"When the asker has an agenda. The police do that. Teachers and doctors, too. Now you're doing it. I don't, and that's why they trust me. I know you're my boss, Dr. Miller, but things in the hills aren't that simple—who's boss and who's not. If somebody's working or not, if a little girl is happy or sad. It's not black and white here. It's all gray."

"Call me Marvin."

"You're learning. Now come on. Try not to look so scared."

"I'm not scared."

"All right, then. Whatever it is, try not to look it. Especially in their home."

Marvin nodded, and followed her across the dirt to the worn three-step rise to the porch. The oak slats were grayed by weather and surprisingly smooth, years of tread having rounded the edges and rubbed splinters away. A broom leaned against the screen door. Wire and string mended the old mesh to keep bugs out. Hattie rapped on the warped door frame.

"Yoo-hoo," she said. "Anybody home?"

Jo opened the door. "Mommy's coming," she said. "You-uns can set in the front room."

Hattie and Marvin stepped into a kitchen with a red Formica table, trimmed by a metal band, and six chairs. A small Frigidaire hummed beside a single-basin sink. The wall held a faded reproduction of the Last Supper. Marvin nodded to himself, appreciating the Christian element, the general cleanliness, and the presence of running water.

Jo led them to the front room, where a couch with broad flat arms faced two easy chairs. The furniture was old and worn. A plaited oval rug lay on the floor. The walls held four black-and-white photographs of babies, and two color pictures depicting Jo in first and second grades. A bare bulb dangled overhead. A child's crib with high sides sat in the corner.

Marvin looked inside the crib. A slender ten-year-old boy wearing a cloth diaper lay on his back, his face turned to the side. He breathed through his mouth. Drool ran from his mouth to a wet area on the bare mattress. The boy's head was misshapen, three times the normal size, its weight preventing him from moving. The plates of the skull had never fused and two were distinctly visible, rising like flat islands from the pale skin. The flesh of his forehead was stretched so tightly that the bottom of each eyelid was pulled over his eyes, rendering him blind.

Jo stroked his arm. His fingers clenched spasmodically like a baby trying to cling. "Hey, Big Billy," she said. "Hey, Big Billy." The boy's coo ended in a gasping wheeze due to pressure on his windpipe from elongated muscles in his neck. "Sissy loves you," Jo said.

The odor of a freshly fouled diaper assailed Marvin and he turned away. A woman entered the room, the boy's mother, he surmised—remarkably lithe and pretty, wearing a housecoat.

"Hidy, Rhonda," Hattie said. "It's nice to see you. How're you feeling?"

"Getting my strength back," Rhonda said. "Jo's a blessing. Set down a spell. Want anything to drink? Jo, run get them some water."

Jo obediently departed. Rhonda moved to a rocking chair with a flat pillow tied to the seat.

"Rhonda," Hattie said, "I'd like you to meet Dr. Miller. He works with me."

"Is he a teacher-doctor or a doctor-doctor?"

Marvin glanced at Hattie, confused.

"She means," Hattie said, "MD or professor."

"Neither one," Marvin said.

"He just stayed in school a long time," Hattie said.

"I had a aunt went to the Normal," Rhonda said. "She always said I was smart enough to. But I got married and had my babies."

Marvin was struck by the combination of youth and age in her face—smooth skin and old eyes. She needed sleep. Her dark hair retained the luster of recent childbirth.

"How can I help you?" she said.

Marvin blinked at the question. It was beyond his comprehension that she didn't understand it was his job to help her. The only sound was the raspy breathing of the boy in the crib.

"Big Billy seems like he's doing good," Hattie said.

"The same," Rhonda said. "He don't change. Happy as the day he was born."

"How's the others getting along?"

"They're eating good and sleeping good."

"And your new baby?"

"I can't tell nothing yet," Rhonda said. "But I get scared for her."

"How she might turn out?"

"Yes'm. She's a good baby. They all are. I love them."

"I know you do," Hattie said. "It's a hardship."

"Sometimes I think it's my fault. But they're God's children."

"We all are," Marvin said.

"I can't hardly get my husband to go to church with me." She stared at Marvin. "You think if he did, things might change?"

"I don't know," he said.

"That's the pity of it," Rhonda said. "Nobody does."

The screen door banged and Jo carried in two cups, blue tin with white spots. She offered them handle first and Marvin drank, the sudden cold stunning his gums as if each tooth had popped from its socket.

"Thank you," Hattie said.

"Coldest I ever drank," Marvin said.

"Always is," Rhonda said, her voice tinged with buried pride. "It's from way deep. My husband got a dowser and I'm telling you, that willow switch jumped around like it was alive. He let me hold the stick. It like to pulled my arms off my body, it was drawing so hard."

"And where is your husband?" Marvin said.

"At work. Up to Ohio. He goes there for them factories. Comes home of the weekends."

"That's a long drive," Marvin said.

"He misses his babies. Bible says provide for your own or you ain't no more account than a infidel."

Hattie sipped the water. Small brown slivers floated on top, pieces broken off the dried and hollowed gourd used as a dipper. She mentally added a metal dipper to a list of necessities for the next visit.

"Can I see your baby?" she said.

Rhonda pressed her hands against the rocker arms and pushed herself to her feet, moving with little energy. Marvin studied her, trying to discern if she was physically ill or had been beaten.

"She's in here," Rhonda said, and led them through a doorway off the front room. A twin bed occupied most of the space, two pillows at the head, a quilt neatly folded at the foot. Wish Book pages made a mural on one wall, taped and peeling. In the corner stood a small crib beside a window. Hattie opened the curtains.

"A little sun won't hurt her," she said.

"I know it," Rhonda said. "I close it of the night so nothing will get her."

"Do you have screens?" Marvin said.

Hattie pursed her lips and gave him a quick head shake of disapproval. Rhonda frowned as if the question made no sense.

"I seen a old broke-tail cat at the edge of the woods," she said. "They say a cat will suck the life out of a baby so I keep this room shut."

"My opinion," Hattie said, "the dogs'll keep it away."

"That's what my husband says. But I laid in here all one night thinking what in case they get to running a rabbit, or chasing after a neighbor dog in heat."

The room was warm and stuffy, the floors clean, no scent of mildew or old laundry. Marvin peered into the crib, where a baby lay, eyes wide, staring at the oblong of light streaming between the floral curtains. The file had said the baby was ten months old but it looked small enough to be undernourished, and he wondered how big a man the father was. The baby's hair was light brown, carefully brushed around her head as if trying to form a halo.

Hattie waved her hand before the baby's face, gauging reaction. None came and she moved her hand closer until her fingers were a few inches away. The pupils of the baby's eyes contracted but didn't refocus on the motion.

"Rolled over on her own?" Hattie said.

Rhonda shook her head. She hated anyone seeing her baby. As long as she kept it in the bedroom and stayed nearby, nobody could ever judge. Deep inside, Rhonda knew something was wrong with Bessie.

"You care if I touch her?" Hattie said.

Rhonda shook her head. The fear blared through her body like a mine blast, down the length of her limbs and bounced back into her chest. She knew she wouldn't sleep that night.

Marvin watched Hattie gently adjust the baby so her face was aimed their way. She had the chubby cheeks of a breast-fed child. The eyes were pale brown, nearly gold, tinged with green. Her brows were long and pale, arching around the outer edges. He had never seen a prettier set of eyes, but it was like looking at the flat dull expression of a cow. He abhorred his own fascination.

"She's a pretty baby," Hattie said. "You're taking right good care of her."

Rhonda turned her head to the window, her face glistening with tears. She made no sound or motion. Through the window a jaybird's raucous call marred the air. A chicken pecked the ground and strolled away as if recalling an important task. The woods were thick with shadowed green, and Rhonda wished she were in them, walking animal trails until they faded into the brush and she was lost, could stay lost for good. She wished Tucker was home. She wished these state people would hurry and leave so she could lie down and sleep. Most of all she wished her next baby wouldn't have anything wrong with it. She heard Hattie ask about the other two kids.

"Upstairs," Rhonda said. "Jo'll show you. I'm going to stay with Bessie. She might need me."

Hattie and Marvin followed Jo up a narrow staircase. The first step was low and the rest of the risers were uneven.

At the top of the steps Jo made a hard right along a hall that led to a closed door. She opened it and stepped inside a room with three beds.

Hattie pointed to the beds as she spoke to Marvin in low tones.

"That's Ida over there. She's five. This is Velmey. She's three and a half."

"Are they . . ." Marvin's voice trailed off. He was aware of Jo listening, unsure of how to proceed.

Hattie nodded curtly. The five-year-old was overweight and asleep, her plump hands clean, her sheets fresh. Velmey's bed was in a corner and she leaned against the wall, propped by pillows on each side holding her in place. She smiled and Marvin realized it was the first smile he'd seen since arriving. Her milk teeth were still coming in, each in its place, none misaligned or crooked. Saliva ran down her chin and Jo wiped it with a scrap of red cotton.

"She can't help it," Jo said.

"Is there anything you want," Hattie said. "Anything I can get you."

"I wish Daddy was here all the time."

"Of course you do. But he has to work. I mean anything you'd like to have for yourself. A dress or new shoes or a barrette. Anything at all, if you had your druthers."

"Daddy took me to town and I seen a calendar in a store."

"A calendar," Marvin said. "So you know what day it is and how long till your daddy comes home?"

"No," Jo said. "I know the days and I can count. I learned all that at school."

"Then why do you want a calendar?" he said.

"It had a picture on it of a pond. I like me a pond."

Marvin glanced about the room. There was nothing on the walls except scuff marks and water stains. The only window had three planks nailed across the bottom panes. He assumed it prevented the children from falling out.

"Is there anything you need to tell me?" Hattie said.

Jo frowned and shrugged.

"If it's something you don't want Dr. Miller to know about, he can leave."

Jo shook her head, staring at the floor, moving one foot back and forth. Her daddy had sanded the edges of the peeled-up paint. She liked how soft it felt under her feet.

"There is something, isn't there," Hattie said.

Jo nodded, still staring at the floor.

"What is it, child? Is it about your sisters?"

"It's about Mommy."

Hattie squatted and leaned close.

"You can tell me," she said.

"Mommy sings a song a lot. To the baby. 'Amazing Grace.'"

"It's a church song."

"I know that," Jo said. She lifted her face to Hattie, the dark eyes trusting and fretful. "But I don't know what grace is. It's bothersome to me, the not knowing."

Hattie rocked back on her heels, unable to answer. She'd never thought about it.

"We need to talk with your mom a little more," she said. "Maybe you can tell your sisters about the calendar."

"But what's grace?"

"You," Hattie said. "The way you take care of these babies. And you're amazing."

Jo nodded, her expression brighter. Hattie and Marvin left the room, closing the door behind them. They heard a bolt lock slide into place, heard Jo's excited murmuring to her sisters.

Marvin lowered his voice as they stood in the narrow hall.

"We have got to do something," he said.

"Not much we can do," Hattie said. "Give them clothes and blankets."

"That room is like a jail cell."

"It's to protect the kids."

"It's unsanitary."

"The kids are clean," Hattie said. "The house is clean."

"That little girl in there is taking care of them."

"No law against that. I took care of my brothers and sisters when I was little. Didn't hurt me."

"It's not the same," Marvin said. "And you know it."

"What I know is they got it rough, rougher than they deserve. My job is to check on the well-being of the children. I believe they are cared for and not lacking. The father works.

The mother is down. Anybody would be. But this family is trying."

"This family is a retard factory is what it is. And this home is unsuitable. I won't stand for it."

He descended the steps. Years ago, Hattie deduced that she couldn't help everyone or allow her compassion to generate too much closeness with clients. The solution was to pick a few particular cases and carefully monitor them. She'd chosen Jo for special attention and now she had to protect the child from the very system intended to assist her.

Hattie went downstairs, hoping to talk sense into Marvin before he insulted Rhonda. If he did, Rhonda would never allow Hattie back in the house. Rhonda held her baby, standing beside Big Billy's crib. The tan planes of her face were drawn tight with tension as if her skin was a web constricting her head. A thick vein pulsed visibly in her neck.

"The state will take good care of your children," Marvin said.

"No," Rhonda said.

"It'll be much easier for you and your family."

"No."

"You can visit them any time you like."

"No, no, no."

"I understand you don't want to hear this, but it really is best."

"No."

"You need to cease relations with your husband."

"You mean leave him?" Rhonda's voice was rising. "Leave my husband?"

Hattie moved slowly forward, arms spread, palms open and aimed upward—posing no threat. Such a posture had proven effective in worse situations.

"Rhonda," she said. "You're a good mother. Your kids belong with you."

"He said to leave."

"No," Marvin said. "What I'm saying is that you and your husband need to stop having babies."

Rhonda's face twitched in numerous places. Her eyes widened, then shut.

"My opinion," Hattie said, "there's another way of going about this business."

"No, there's not," Marvin said. "I'm getting a court order to take these kids."

"No," Rhonda said. "Please."

"Until then," he said, "don't you get pregnant again."

"How?"

"Dr. Miller," Hattie said. "I believe Rhonda and me need to talk alone. Woman to woman."

Marvin had no desire to discuss the particulars of Rhonda's intimate life. He'd made his decision. He stepped outside, waited briefly on the porch, then walked to the car. A breeze rustled the high boughs of the nearest trees. The wind ceased and the air was silent. He heard his own breath, felt his heart beating, imagined that he could hear the blood rushing through his veins.

He calmed himself and slowly swiveled on his heels. The trees seemed to separate themselves from their collective growth and he could see the slick bark of a sycamore, the concave strips of birch, an oak surrounded by open ground, and the liquidy stands of pine. Near a hand-dug drain ditch grew a low redbud flanked by dogwood. The shaded loam of the hills held lady's slipper, jack-in-the-pulpit, and trillium—delicate and rare. At one time he'd considered studying botany instead of psychology. He could be working in a greenhouse or as a florist. He'd be carefully digging up wildflowers for transplant into richer soil, better for thriving. Maybe it would be the same for these children.

Hattie came outside, her face stark and blunt. She got into the car and started the engine, dreading the long drive back to the office. She rode the brake off the hill. Rocks bounced against the floorboards and she steered carefully to straddle the deep gully left by rain in the middle of the road. She felt like crying, like quitting her job, like chewing out her boss. Instead, she focused on the task at hand, driving the rough blacktop that was brittle at the edge. She reminded herself of past successes—the boy who'd gotten his high school equivalency diploma, the teenage girl who'd fled her abusive father, the child who brushed his teeth for the first time at age nine. These small triumphs couldn't offset the rage she felt toward Marvin.

After the state people left, Rhonda swaddled the baby in her crib, and checked on Big Billy who acknowledged her by grasping once with his hand. She climbed the steps to the second floor. Her chest felt like a shaken snow globe. She lay on Jo's bed and clutched her tightly, listening to all the children breathe together, the slow inhalations producing a hum that lulled her into calmness.

She'd lied to Hattie and feared being caught. Her husband didn't work in a steel mill. He drove loads of moonshine to Ohio for a man named Beanpole. Tucker was due home today. She began to pray for his safety. The prayers couldn't quell the swirling miasma of her thoughts. Two miscarriages, then water-brained Billy produced cracks in her heart like an old plate banged too often on the table. Jo's birth renewed her faith. Each ensuing pregnancy had been nine months of fervent hope ending in dismay.

Doctors in Lexington had found nothing wrong with her. After Ida and Velmey, her husband reluctantly succumbed to the long drive for an afternoon of testing. He was healthy, too. It wasn't his different-colored eyes or either one's family. They ate as well as anyone on the hill. She'd not undergone any odd illness while big with child. The doctors said it was bad luck.

More than anything she wanted to give Tucker a boy. He deserved a normal son. She'd done everything the doctors said. She rested daily and listened to the old women who'd raised ten kids in the Depression, losing three on average. They said God always had a plan. Rhonda couldn't see what this plan was other than a punishment. She loved the babies with every cell of her being but it always felt one-sided. They were too bad off to love her back.

The state man's threat to steal her family enlivened her as if doused by ice water. The leaden fatigue of her despair evaporated. Something inside her unlocked. She could feel it in her hips and bowels and chest as if a switch had been thrown at a powerhouse and she knew her next child would be a boy, healthy as a dog.

Chapter Six

Later that afternoon the sound of a car engine woke Jo from a nap. She hurried downstairs, out the door, and ran to her father. Tucker squatted, knowing she'd leap. He caught her easily, standing and spinning in a circle, holding her tight. Jo's legs swung nearly straight, her dress billowing, hair flying. She arched her back and tipped her head, smiling and laughing. Tucker set her on the trunk of the car.

"How's my sugar-pie honey-child?" Tucker said.

"Happy now, Daddy," she said.

"I believe you growed while I was gone."

She stiffened her back and lifted her chin.

"Yes, I surely do," he said. "Maybe two, three inches. Why, you're bigger than me."

"I'm setting on the car, Daddy."

He gave her a paper sack of lemon drops, her favorite penny candy.

"These are grow-pills," he said, "take one at a time."

She tore open the folded bag and slid a yellow pellet in her mouth. Tucker searched his pockets in an elaborate fashion and pulled forth a red velvet ribbon, one side darker than the other.

"You take and put that in your hair," he said.

"Thank you, Daddy."

"Now tell me who's been up here today."

"That state lady and a man with her. How'd you know?"

"Seen the tracks, Jo. Look there."

Jo followed his pointing finger to the narrow furrows of tread in the dry dirt driveway. Her daddy could see everything and anything. He could name a bird by its egg, a tree by its leaf, and knew the star pictures in the sky. The lemon drop was half dissolved, and she wondered if it would still make her grow. More than anything she wanted to have babies of her own.

Tucker gathered two bags of groceries from the backseat. He encircled his daughter with his other arm and carried her across the yard, tired from sixteen hours of driving. He was thirsty and his shoulders were sore. He placed the bags on the kitchen table, let Jo slide down his body to the floor, and winked at his wife, who stood smiling shyly. He leaned into Big Billy's crib and slid his hands gently beneath his enlarged head. Big Billy cooed from his father's touch. Tucker lifted his son's head, rotated it in the air, and settled it on the mattress. Big Billy now faced the opposite way, though his body had barely moved. The side of his head was damp with sweat, the hair matted to the sections of his skull. Tucker blotted the perspiration with a handkerchief and finger-combed his son's hair.

In his own bedroom he stroked Bessie's tiny arm and kissed her, then went upstairs to kiss Ida and Velmey. The road tension begin to fade from his limbs. He went outside to smoke a Lucky and wait for the evening birds. Rhonda joined him, a couple not yet thirty with five children, sitting in rockers on the porch like they were already old folks. She never asked about his moonshine runs. She didn't want to know the perils he faced to provide for the family.

Neither minded the silence, both happy to be near each other. Jo came outside and climbed onto Tucker's lap. After a while Rhonda asked her to go check on the babies. Jo kissed her father and left.

"State came," Rhonda said.

He nodded and continued to rock.

"It was two this time. The man . . ."

She let her voice trail away, not wanting to hurt him with the information that had left her breathless.

"They was two?" Tucker said.

"The regular lady and a man. Some kind of doctor."

He nodded and blew a smoke ring that dissipated in the easy breeze.

"They say anything?"

"Said for me not to have no more kids. Said he was going to take the babies."

"What?" Tucker stopped rocking. "What did he say?"

"We ain't supposed to have no more kids. He's aiming to take the babies."

"And do what with them?"

"I don't know."

"How long ago did they leave here?"

"About a hour, maybe a little more."

"Goddamn," he said. "Goddamn sons-of-bitches."

"I don't like that talk, even if it is over the babies."

"I know it, Rhonda. I'm sorry."

He snapped the cigarette into the yard and walked to his car. His sudden anger found focus as he drove off the hill. Tucker seldom took chances but today he was breaking the most important rule—using the run-car for a personal matter on main roads. His old truck would never catch up with the state people. The run-car was rear-ended like a hearse, could haul concrete block up a creek bed. He pushed the engine hard, circumventing Morehead as best he could. He drove on dirt roads, and had to catch a piece of highway on the way out of town. It was a gamble he didn't like to take, but the alternatives were fire roads or logging trails and they'd add more time than he could spare.

He passed a truck and two cars, swerving around them as if they were mirages standing immobile in the road. He slowed twice—for the single-lane covered bridge over the Little Sandy River, and again when he came barreling around a curve to confront two mules pulling a wagon that listed to one side. He didn't want to rile the team and pitch the old driver off the seat. After the wagon went by, he pushed the speed over a hundred on the few straight stretches, double-clutching to downshift through the turns. He knew every pothole in the road, every tree branch that swept low, every blind curve and entrance lane. Tucker drove without thought, operating on instinct, holding the steering wheel lightly, trusting the machine to obey the slightest twitch of his hands.

He slowed at the edge of Salt Lick. Suspended on two chains from a tree was a car door advertising a used car lot, the paint faded and blotched with rust. He ran high and heavy in second, the engine struggling under restraint. The main road was the only street in town. Salt Lick had one cop who went off duty at sundown, still an hour away. Tucker headed for the gas station on the going-toward-Lexington side of town. Next to the pumps was a diner known for possessing the biggest window around, although it was actually five panes of glass connected by metal strips. A red neon sign said "EAT" in large letters. Amid the dimming dusk, light from the diner spilled onto the cement lot, cracked and heaved from frost. Three unoccupied vehicles were visible. One was newer than the rest, with plates from Franklin County, the state capital.

Tucker parked behind the gas station on a dirt lot covered with car parts and drums of old motor oil. He left the car and circled the building, staying in the shade until he could see the front. Inside the diner a workingman wearing a cap, flannel shirt, and dungarees drank coffee at the counter. Past him was a man in a dress shirt sitting with a woman. Tucker studied the sight lines and took a position beneath a cluster of cedar. The strong smell made his eyes water but he was hidden from view, able to see the diner and car, the ground soft from dead brown needles. He had his pistol and knife.

As the sun slid into the tree line, light leaked out of the land. The neon sign glowed orange against the purple sky. He recalled coming here as a teenager with a group of boys to admire the big window. They'd stood around the parking lot, talking rough, arguing about how the glass was delivered during construction. None of them had eaten in a restaurant and they stayed outside. Each boy took a leak in the weeds before leaving. Tucker wondered if he was hunkered down in the same spot where he'd pissed several years before. The glass wall lacked its previous wonder. Now it had cracks covered in tape, the grand panes greasy from exhaust fumes and grit, stained at the top from rain. He watched the couple eating.

During her twenties, Hattie had developed a kind of intuition, which alerted her when the attention of men needed fending off. She considered Marvin a broken sad sack who relied on his job to feel good. He disgusted her with the accidental brushes of her arm, the clandestine glances at her bosom. Hattie's deflections were a case of casual ignoring, as if she hadn't noticed. Instead of getting the message, he'd increased his efforts.

In her thirty-four years of walking the earth Hattie had kissed one boy and didn't like it, one girl and did—and wound up so distraught by the conflict that she joined church with an aggression that lasted six months until she quit. Like most women she preferred the social company of women. She didn't participate in their gossip, but studied their arms, their necks, their ankles, and their lips. Hattie knew she had a left-handed turn. It was in the family—her mannish aunt had moved off and never visited. Though often surrounded by people, Hattie felt dreadfully alone. At night she drank sherry, purchased at three different stores to conceal her habit. She read paperback novels that cost thirty-five cents. She imagined herself not as the scantily clad women on the covers, but as the men who rescued them. Her legs and stomach tingled. She knew the problem, if it indeed counted as a problem, and had no idea what to do about it, stuck in a conservative town with a public job.

Marvin drank coffee and ate pie with the family's folder open in front of him like a menu.

"Hydrocephaly," he said.

He repeated the word three times. Hattie gave a quick shake of her head at the first two, then quit responding.

"Hydrocephaly," he said again. "No record of a shunt to drain the fluid. By all rights that baby should've died. Why didn't it? That's what I'd like to know. And these others, there's no diagnosis. They didn't look like Downs to me."

"I don't believe they are Downs," she said. "Ida is alert, just sleeps a lot. Good focus. She can copy complicated designs from scraps of cloth."

"An idiot quilt maker. What about the other two?"

"Too soon to know with the baby. The other one, Velmey, she's got limited motor skills. But they're all physically healthy as a mule."

"There's no pattern," he said.

"None that we can see."

Hattie accepted a refill of pop to wash down the last of her sandwich. She wished she'd ordered french fries, but knew they'd upset her stomach. Her head hurt like a hog bite. She tore open a packet of BC aspirin powder, dumped it into a glass of water, and watched the swirling crystals dissolve. It was bitter as a peach pit but she drank it in one long swallow.

"Hydrocephaly," he said.

"Please stop staying that," she said.

"Why didn't they shunt it?" Marvin said.

"What I heard," Hattie said, "they thought the baby would die so they didn't drain the liquid. Then he lived."

"What kind of doctor does that?"

"A granny-woman."

"What?"

"Mountain midwife. Beulah Tolliver. She delivered a few generations on that hill."

"Thought they were done with that."

"Mostly they are," she said. "There's two doctors in the county, both in Morehead. One charges high, the other won't leave the town limits. Women in the hills use a granny-woman. If there's complications, she gets hold of a doctor. In this case, she waited a day, and the doctor showed up two days later."

"Are you blaming medical personnel?"

"People don't have phones. The roads are bad, and not enough doctors. Most of the time, it works out fine."

"But not this time."

"I don't judge," she said. "That's a habit you might think about taking up."

"What's that supposed to mean?"

"What it sounds like, Marvin. I can't fix what already happened. My job is to try and make things easier on the family."

"A mother with severe melancholia," he said. "An absent father. A house full of freaks. I was afraid I'd find another room with a bearded lady and an alligator boy."

Hattie felt like a cat with a hair ball the size of a pinecone. She wanted to slap him in the face and go back to Frankfort alone. She clenched her teeth and spoke in a quiet tone.

"Those kids are all that mother and little girl have. There isn't a problem, Marvin."

"It's coming, Hattie. They come of age, they'll start rubbing on the furniture, then on each other."

"You don't know the future."

"Yes, I darn well do. Those kids are coming out of that house or I'll know the reason why. You're either with me on this, or you're not."

"There's no abuse," she said. "No neglect. No grounds for removal from the home."

Marvin grinned inwardly, hearing the urgency in her voice. He had married a woman he didn't love because her father could get him a state job in Frankfort. The old man died and Marvin's career stalled. Now he was stuck with a wife who went to bed mad, woke up mad, and stayed irritable all day. Pretending to glance at the table in contemplation, he appraised Hattie's body. Though she wore loose clothes he'd studied her often enough to know she had a set of heavy lungs beneath her blouse and fine wide flanks. Between Mount Sterling and Winchester there was the Blue Top Motel that would suit his purposes.

He arranged on his face an expression of deep compassion, one he'd copied from a preacher, and shifted his body forward. He placed his hand on hers, the touch of skin sizzling through his body straight to his groin.

"We'll let them kids be," he said. "If that's what you want, we can do that, you and me. First we need to go somewhere private and talk out all the options. I know a place up the road a piece." He bared his teeth in his most alluring smile. "You like gin?"

Hattie's mouth was dry as old leaves. For thirty seconds that felt like weeks, she remained stoic and unmoving as the meaning of his words filtered through her mind. Her job was at stake. The child. The mother. Everything she believed in and worked toward.

"Have to go to the ladies'," she whispered.

She tugged her hand away and stood, hoping the unsteadiness in her legs wasn't evident. She walked the length of the diner, past the freshly scrubbed breakfast bar, the full cups of sugar with their tiny spoons. In the cramped bathroom she held on to the sink as her body shivered. She used several wads of toilet paper to remove every speck of makeup, hoping to make herself less attractive. She felt torn in half. The urge to protect the children conflicted with her own sense of futility and outrage. Reporting Marvin would get her fired. Enduring his desire was no guarantee that he'd leave the family alone. She could put off the inevitable but at a terrible cost.

Hattie felt gripped by one of those Japanese finger cuffs in a Cracker Jack box—paper that tightened as you struggled to free yourself. From the restroom window came the sound of the cook throwing trash in a garbage can and pounding the metal lid tight. She could leave through the kitchen, get in her car, and drive away. She could quit her job, vacate her bleak apartment, and move to Chicago.

Marvin sat with no patience, his desire increasing each time he looked at his watch. He hoped to high heaven she wasn't undergoing a bout of female trouble. Maybe Hattie was adjusting herself, applying a skim of crimson lipstick like the women on magazine covers. He finished his coffee and paid the bill. The waitress left with the workingman, and Marvin felt a pang of envy undercut with anger. He was the one with an education befitting a jacket and tie, creased pants and wing tips, now slightly soiled. He polished them on the back of each calf. He straightened his clothes and strode through the diner and into the dark parking lot. When she emerged from the ladies' room, she'd no doubt hurry his way like a fly to sugar.

Tucker waited in the black shadowed stand of cedar thinking about his brothers. Two were dead, and one may as well be. As boys they'd roamed the hills with burlap pokes and hoes, gathering mayapple and low-billy, and selling them by the ounce. Tucker spent the most time with his older brother Casey. At sixteen Casey had begun digging ginseng, a more valuable plant, and shot a man in the woods over a four-year root as thick as a wrist. He'd gone to prison for murder and emerged addled as a paddle, his left temple dented from a blow by a pipe, one eye missing. Afterward Casey couldn't stay focused enough to clear rock from a road.

Tucker gave their mother money when he could, but Casey took it and got drunk and set fire to a man's chicken house. The man found him eating half-cooked bird, his mouth filled with feathers. The state put him in a lockdown hospital north of Lexington. Tucker visited once with his mother, appalled at living conditions worse than the chickens his brother had killed. Their mother never recovered from the visit, had begun a gradual dwindle to death.

The diner sign flickered and hummed. The man in the suit came outside and leaned on the car. He propped one foot on the bumper, then arranged himself in a casual position as if nothing mattered in the world.

Tucker moved slowly along the tree line, placing the sole of each boot on its edge and easing his foot down, prepared at the slightest sound to stop. He lowered his chin to protect his throat. He didn't blink. Tucker stepped from the trees to the edge of darkness, deliberately scraping his boots.

Marvin turned to the sound, a fragment of his mind thinking Hattie stood behind him, dress unbuttoned and off the shoulder, having slipped outside to surprise him. Seeing the short man in work clothes disappointed Marvin.

"I have important business here," Marvin said. "It doesn't concern you. I'll thank you to travel on."

"Was it you up to Tunnel Cut Holler at a woman's house had five kids today?"

It took Marvin a few seconds to unravel the mountain syntax and make sense of the question. He assumed the man was concerned about ethics, a home visit to a woman alone. Marvin held his tie with one hand and adjusted the half-Windsor knot, a gesture of authority he'd practiced. He squared his shoulders, and cleared his throat. He knew how to talk to people, especially these people.

"Yes," Marvin said. "It was a professional appointment. A female colleague accompanied me."

Tucker stepped into the light, his dual-colored eyes startling Marvin momentarily. Tucker glanced past Marvin at the side of the car. Marvin followed his gaze and in that millisecond Tucker pressed his toes to the earth and sprang forward, the Ka-Bar knife flashing in the moonlight as he stabbed Marvin below the sternum, twisting the knife to puncture a lung and pushing the point into the bottom of his heart. Marvin was unsure what had happened. He felt suddenly weak and not quite able to breathe.

"Help me," he tried to say, but no words issued from his mouth, only blood.

A searing agony swept through his body. He reached for the side mirror and his knees gave out. He slid down the car as if an invisible force pushed him toward the earth. The wall of pain perplexed him because he couldn't feel his body. He closed his eyes, smelling his own urine, his last feelings those of embarrassment.

Tucker watched the man's legs tremble involuntarily, knowing from Korea that it wouldn't last long, that he was bleeding internally. He died without a sound. Tucker turned to leave and saw the woman from the diner standing immobile at the front of the car. He sensed her fear, her stunned disbelief, and something else he could not name.

Hattie had fled the diner through the kitchen, onto its crude loading dock, past the garbage cans, and hurried to her car. In the darkness she hadn't seen Marvin until the short man stepped from the shadows and stabbed him.

"He your husband?" Tucker said.

She shook her head rapidly, dislodging strands of hair that floated like glowing tendrils in the diner's light.

"Fiancée or whatnot?" he said.

She shook her head again.

"But you damn sure knowed him," he said.

She nodded.

"Sorry for the language," he said.

"I didn't like him," she said.

"Then why set down to eat with him?"

"I was hungry," she said.

After combat he'd killed wounded enemy, using his bayonet to save ammunition. But she wasn't wounded and he didn't think she was an enemy. He had never killed a woman and didn't want to start. Lacking protocol or experience, he was unsure how to proceed.

"Say you didn't like him," he said. "How come you to not to?"

"He wanted me to go to a motel with him."

"Was you aiming to do it?"

"No."

"He making you go?"

"Yes. I was trying to get loose of him."

"Well you are now."

They both looked at Marvin.

"Do you know me?" Tucker said.

She shook her head.

"Make sure you don't when the law comes. I got to go."

"What do I do?"

"Say you found him laying this way."

"All right," she said.

"Ain't nobody else was here. Just him. What's your name?"

"Hattie," she said. "Hattie Johnson."

"This your car?"

"Yes."

"I'll remember that."

Tucker stepped into the woods and watched her go back in the diner. He drove slowly, using a network of dirt roads, making a wide arc through two counties to avoid detection. He wondered what kind of doctor the man was. He remembered the Lexington hospital where he'd given blood and urine, answered gobs of questions about his family, and had his eyes examined. He'd thought something was wrong with Rhonda's undercarriage or his nutball sack, but the doctors said the test results were normal. They likened the problem to blending food that tasted good separately but made a terrible mess together, like soup beans and bananas in a single stew.

"It's not your fault," the doctor said.

"Ain't they nothing to do?" Tucker said.

"No, there's no medicine to fix the problem."

"Way I see it," Tucker said, "we're due for a good baby."

"It doesn't work that way."

"How does it work?

"I don't know."

"All those years of schooling," Tucker said, "and none of it took."

He gently helped Rhonda to her feet and they left. She cried for a month of Sundays and the next baby laid her out. Rhonda looked like she'd been sent for and couldn't come, got there and wasn't wanted. But Tucker still yet wanted her, wanted his family, and wanted a regular son.

At the foot of his home hill he parked beneath a willow struggling beside the creek. He climbed the shoulder of the land to his ridge, stopping to listen every thirty yards, but the night was still, his own passage alerting the nocturnal animals to quiet themselves. He studied his house from each direction. He found no sign of man, no car tracks, smelled no cigarettes, saw no flash of moonlight on a gun barrel. Satisfied, he went inside. He carefully lifted Big Billy's head and turned it, then leaned into the crib and brushed his lips along his son's sweaty face.

In his bedroom he removed his boots and clothes, kissed baby Bess, and listened to his wife's steady breathing. He rubbed the silken skin of her hip until she drowsily rolled his way. He held her tight, then began caressing her shoulders and arms, running his fingertips the length of her body from collarbone to calf. Rhonda awakened little by little, as if in sections. She smelled his sweat and smoke. She rolled onto her back and opened her thighs. When he was inside, she clasped her arms across his shoulders and dug her nails into the meat of his back. They moved with a steady rhythm, neither talking, aware of each other's breath, the bed creaking. Her tiny grunting gasps increased. She wrapped her legs around the back of his knees as he arched his back, propped on his forearms, his head tipped like a drowning man seeking the surface of water. They finished and he collapsed. She stroked the back of his head, feeling his muscles relax. He fell asleep, a quick hard nap, and jerked awake fully alert. His movement pulled her from the edge of her own slumber. She glanced at the baby, who hadn't stirred in her basket.

"They'll not bother you no more," he whispered.

"Who?"

"Them people here today."

"I couldn't stand to lose my little ones."

"I know it," he said. "Ain't nobody taking them."

She wept a few minutes, the longest time in years, and he felt the wetness against his face, understanding that she felt relief, not sorrow. That diner woman was brave but Rhonda was tough as a buffalo, and these few seconds of crying filled him with lust. He began moving inside her again and afterward she dropped into sleep like a bucket down a well.

He rose and tugged his pants on and went to the living room. He moved a chair beside the crib and tucked his finger into Big Billy's small curled hand. He wondered if his son dreamed. His own dreams were nightmares of combat, but Big Billy had spent all his life in this room. He had nothing to dream about except lying in bed.

Tucker propped an arm on the rung of the crib, pressed his forehead to the maple rail, and spoke.

"Won't be long and you'll be growed up enough to go fishing. We'll use crawdads for bait. They got two little pincers and they run backward. Fish love them like a bee loves a flower. You take and jab one on a hook, and it'll get hit by all manner of fish. The trick is to pull one pincer off. It'll still fight but not much and the fish'll hit it harder. They's some to cut both pincers off but that don't seem right to me. I'd hate to be done that way. The golden rule is made out of gold so you can keep track of it even at night and it goes for everything down to a crawdad.

"My daddy, he grew us a garden that raccoons got into. Daddy got tired of them messing his garden up, eating the best. What he done was decide that half the garden was for him and the other half for raccoons. He run a string around the garden and hung tin cans that'd rattle if they got touched. Then he slept out there with a twenty-two and when them cans woke him up, he'd look to see where the coon was. If it was on the coon's side of the garden Daddy let him alone. But if ary a coon came over on Daddy's side, he shot it. Next day he'd skin it out and hang its hide on a stick. He done that two or three times a week. Them coons figured out which was their side of the garden and stayed out of Daddy's.

"Every animal I ever knowed is a big bunch smarter than folks think they are. We walk around on our hind legs and can do things like drive a car but that don't make us special. For one thing, we can't fly. I mean we can in a airplane but I seen them wreck. Ain't a bird in its whole life ever got hurt landing. I'd like to see that, wouldn't you? Some big old crow coming down to eat a run-over squirrel on the road and not getting it right and crash-landing in the ditch. When you get old enough, you and me'll go out and set us some crow bait on the road and wait till it happens. I'll teach you how to roll a cigarette while we're waiting. A man's got to learn that or he won't never have no way of knowing how good a store-bought is. I got a line on getting a tobacco bed from the state for a cash crop. If you help me with it, you'll get some of the auction money for your ownself.

"Running shine is a hard way to make an easy living and they ain't no better feeling than outfoxing a lawman. One time I was running heavy and full. A deputy was set up waiting and pulled in right behind me and I floored it, was flying low. I never let up on that gas pedal. Went through two crossroads with no trouble, hit me a dirt road shortcut I knew about, and slung the gravel-rock. That deputy stayed on me. I could see his lights but I knowed about a tight turn coming up. I hit it hard, sliding sideways, hoping not to blow a tire. That old rig did me right and I bounced up on two side wheels and fishtailed my ass back on the road and made it to a old wood bridge nobody used no more on account of rotten struts. I stopped halfway over the river. I was out of the state and my heart was jumping around inside my clothes like a squirrel in a pillow sack. I got out and checked the tires. Two rims was bent and I'd lost some tie rods. I figured I could make it to a filling station where a feller I knew would fix me up and keep quiet about it.

"That deputy car came over the bridge and stopped right behind me. He got out, biggest man I ever did see. Some kind of giant. He lit hisself a cigarette and looked at me a spell. I knowed I was safe from him as a lawman, but not as a regular man. He could kick my ass so high I'd have to pull my shirt up to take a shit. What he done was lean on my car and tell me they had a new steering called rack-and-pinion that would keep me out of the ditch line. I asked what did he care for, and he said he thought I wasn't going to make it on that curve. His job was to stop the runners but he didn't want nobody dying on him. We got to talking. He had had four kids and worked another job, and only got assigned shine duty twice a month. I asked if he knew when he was working next. We sat right there on that bridge and worked us out a deal. I got to drive through his county when he was on duty. We didn't tell each other our names, but we shook hands and I always called him Flattop off the funny pages. He was all right. He was a family man first, lawman second, and when you have kids of your own, you'll be the same way, my opinion. He got killed in a shoot-out and I had to find me a new way across the river.

"Son, I'm getting plumb wore down from the past week and have to hit the sack here in a minute. But they's one more thing I been meaning to tell you. It's about squirrels. Took me a long time to figure out how smart they are. Many's the acorn I found with two little holes in the same place. Same size holes, same place on the nut. I started opening them nuts up. Them holes were right where the meatiest part of the nut was at. Squirrels know it. I matched them holes to a squirrel's teeth. It was a perfect fit. They figured out where to bite that nut to get the most. And right now, up in some oak tree in the woods, they's a daddy squirrel telling his boy how to do it. Same as me and you. Daddy loves you, Big Billy. Daddy loves you."

He kissed his son and went to bed. Rhonda pressed herself to Tucker and slid her feet between his, glad he was home. Their bodies warmed each other.

Upstairs Jo lay curled on her side, knees pulled to her chest. Her daddy's voice downstairs had awakened her. He talked to Big Billy every night. She looked at the small section of night sky visible through the top of her window. Once she'd seen a falling star and her mother told her it was an angel smiling. The flash of light was too quick for Jo to smile back and she worried that she'd been rude. She watched for the angel's return, afraid she'd upset it into staying away. As her eyelids closed, she thought about the calendar Hattie would bring her. Maybe angels liked ponds, too.

1965

Chapter Seven

The southerners who'd moved to Ohio and Michigan for jobs preferred the moonshine of home, and Beanpole's business thrived from all the runs to the north. Tucker and the other drivers returned with cases of government whiskey that Beanpole bootlegged by the half pint in dry counties. He secretly funded every political campaign and donated to many churches. His web of bribery spanned two states and included sheriffs, mayors, police officers, jailers, magistrates, two doctors, three judges, and several ministers. He'd never been arrested.

In his spare time, Beanpole fooled with dogs—raising, breeding, and trading them. He made sure they were dewormed and free of mange, their coats glossy and eyes bright. Periodically he cleared them of ticks. His wife said if he'd treated their children the way he treated dogs, the kids would've turned out better and not moved so far away. Beanpole didn't respond. They had four daughters who did what girls did—get courted by lunkheads, marry the worst of the lot, and visit on Sundays with a passel of little lunkheads.

The kids had moved because of his occupation as an outlaw, not poor fathering on his part. He didn't think nine miles was all that far away anyway.

A year ago he watched a Jack Russell tear into a possum's tail, which had the long skinny appearance of a snake. The dog took a deep hold, shredding the meat and hair. Most dogs leaped about barking, careful to remain out of striking range of a snake, a trait that displayed good sense. Beanpole caught a garter snake and threw it into a walled pen with the Jack. The terrier tore it to pieces. Beanpole thought long and hard about matters, then traded four truck tires, a Bowie knife, and six boxes of thirty-eight-caliber cartridges for a pair of purebred German shepherd pups. He theorized that a crossbreed with the Jack Russells would make an ideal snake dog—the shepherd half would corral the serpents, and the Jack part would take over, willing to burrow into the earth after its prey. He planned on selling them and had a name picked out: Viper Wipers.

He contacted a buddy who made a living from selling rattlesnakes to Pentecostals that needed them for church services. Beanpole bought the man's extras, nonvenomous snakes that wandered into his traps. He spent months training the shepherd pups to treat snakes like their own private flock, an elaborate undertaking with carefully designed pens. It hadn't worked out as well as he'd hoped—the pups tried to play with the snakes, then barked for hours until both groups resolved to ignore each other.

When the adult shepherd went into heat, Beanpole put her in a pen with a male Jack Russell. The funniest thing he'd ever seen on God's green earth was the little Jack humping on a dog four times its size. Afterward, the shepherd retaliated with a vicious attack. Beanpole wasn't quick enough to separate them and the Jack sustained a wound so severe he had to put the dog down. He considered it a good sign. The eventual crossbred pups had a fearless father and a ferocious mother.

Beanpole had married early and well, and still loved his wife. She'd started out big and wore weight well, only her feet and hands still small. Beanpole didn't mind—he weighed three hundred fifty pounds himself. Despite advancing into their forties and being grandparents, they still made the feather tick bust a seam once or twice a month, last night being one. As a result, Angela was in a cheery mood at breakfast. They ate eggs and side meat, mopping the grease with cathead biscuits, washing it down with coffee strong enough to float a rock. He tried to assume a pleasant tone, knowing she'd recognize it for what it was—a precursor to something she wouldn't like.

"You got anybody to go visit today?" he said.

"Why? Some fancy lady from Morehead coming by?"

"Now, no," he said, playing along. "But if you stood gone through the evening I might could squeeze one in."

"Ain't you done squeezed out yet?"

"I am," he said. "I surely am. You seen to that last night."

"I'll not have that talk at the table."

He nodded and sipped coffee. He'd never fully comprehended what was allowed at the table and what was not.

"I got to see a man today," he said.

"Here?"

He nodded.

"I don't like that," she said. "Not one bit."

He sipped coffee. She'd grown up with brothers rough as cobs and twice witnessed gunfights, one in the house and another in the yard. He'd sworn years ago never to bring his business home.

"It's a tricky situation," he said.

"Say it's tricky."

"Yeah-huh," he said. "Not bad tricky. But not easy, either. I got to work something out that might take a spell of talking. I don't want to meet in the woods."

"He from here?"

Beanpole nodded.

"Why not go to his house, then?" she said.

"Well," he said, then tapered off, feeling bad about not telling her the why, and worse for the reason.

"I can't," he said.

"Say you can't?"

"Can't do it."

He looked away from her face, still lovely in the light. Patience had always been her chief virtue, and his business had certainly put it to trial, but at times he thought Angela's patience could grind a man down as sure as sandy water.

She heaved a sigh of disapproval, wondering if last night's antics had been deliberately calculated to soften her up. If so, it worked. Her husband was the smartest man she'd ever met, as smart as her, which was unusual. He'd never struck her or the babies, kept food on the table and gave each daughter a down payment on land. Angela drove her own car, the only woman at church who did. She sat with the sick, cooked for the bereaved, and drove old folks to the town doctor. Generating goodwill was her contribution to her husband's business. Anybody could get angry and tip off the law. The problem was that the law would tell Beanpole, forcing him to retaliate, which would start trouble for everyone.

"I'll find somewhere to go," she said. "Is they anybody in particular I ort to stay away from today?"

"Naw," he said. "It ain't like that."

"That's a blessing."

"I appreciate it."

Angela stacked the dishes noisily, and gave him a quick sharp look that meant he was to wash them in her absence, even though she'd have to wash them again later. If he intended to run her out of her own home, he'd pay a price. She changed clothes, hearing water in the sink, and when she returned to the kitchen the plates lay damp and shiny on an old cotton towel, not as dirty as she'd expected. Angela found him sitting on the porch, staring at the sky with no more care than a bluebird in a bush. She patted his shoulder.

"Don't get shot, Ananias," she said.

"Ain't as bad as all that."

"You don't know."

"Maybe not, but I'm pretty sure."

"All right then."

He considered himself damn lucky in the wife department, even if she did call him by his given name. After she drove away, grim-faced before the dire responsibility of the steering wheel, he armed himself with a revolver. He loaded a shotgun and set it just inside the doorway, out of sight but easily reachable. He sat on the porch to wait. The house was pleasantly quiet, the shaded porch still chilly at midday. An hour later he heard the engine of a vehicle. As the truck swung into view, the driver honked twice to alert the house. Beanpole peered at the windshield to make sure there was only one man.

After Tucker's last run to northern Ohio, he'd dutifully left the money with an intermediary, Beanpole's second cousin, a grass widow who smoked a pipe. She told Tucker that Beanpole wanted to see him on Friday. For the next two days, Tucker wondered what he wanted. Maybe a new run-route to Chicago or Pittsburgh. Or maybe the sons-of-bitches in West Virginia were encroaching into Kentucky and trouble was coming. Tucker carried his gun and knife just in case.

The flat part of the yard beside Beanpole's house had a gravel parking area, an extravagance Tucker had never seen outside of town. Shingles covered the roof instead of the usual tarpaper. The yard held a wooden swing suspended from a yoked scaffold. On the porch Beanpole sat in a rocking chair reinforced by wire against his weight.

Tucker stepped from the cab amid a cacophony of penned dogs that howled their warnings. Nobody could sneak up on Beanpole's house. Tucker stood in front of his truck and faced the house. With slow and deliberate movements, he removed a Lucky from his shirt pocket and lit it with the other hand. He tucked the Zippo away and let both arms dangle, showing empty hands. A slight breeze blew the cigarette smoke back in his face. He squinted, keeping them open as he watched Beanpole. In Korea he'd seen men die in the time of a single blink.

"You coming up here?" Beanpole said.

"Not yet, no."

"What are you waiting on, a letter from the governor?"

Beanpole gushed out the stream of laughter he used to put folks at ease. Tucker didn't react. Beanpole let his mirth subside, remembering that Tucker's job placed him in contact with strangers who might be robbers, killers, or hijackers. Beanpole rose and stepped to the edge of the porch. He carefully placed both his big-knuckled hands on the railing.

Tucker nodded once and walked to the house, flicking the focus of his vision between Beanpole's eyes and his hands. Both men knew the other was armed, and each was aware that the other knew it, too. But one would have to draw first. Tucker flicked his cigarette away. He kicked the bottom plank of the oak steps to remove dust from his boots, a sign of respect, even though he had no intention of entering the house.

"Anybody else here?" he said.

"Old lady's off I don't know where."

"They a man up in the woods drawed down on me right now?"

"If they was," Beanpole said, "I wouldn't tell you, would I?"

"No, but if you lied, I'd know."

"You can cipher out a man lying?"

Tucker nodded. Beanpole studied on that, wondering if it was true. Maybe Tucker's funny-colored eyes gave him an extra ability.

"All right," Beanpole said. He patted the enormous belly swelling the front flap of his overalls. "This here ain't fat, it's a shed for my tool. Now which one's a lie?"

"You not being fat."

"Well, you got me, Tuck. You damn sure do. Caught me lying like a rug. Now why don't you come up here and set down."

Tucker remained in the yard, gauging angles. Beanpole had the advantage of elevation, but he'd have to shoot over the railing, which would slow him down and throw off his aim. Tucker figured he could fire from his hip before Beanpole had a chance.

"I'm all right where I'm at," Tucker said.

"They's something we need to talk about."

"Figured that."

Another minute passed. The sound of the dogs diminished, then picked up, rolling in waves across the earth, the low-pitched moan of the hounds steady beneath the other dogs. The quick sharp cries of a terrier echoed back from the end of the ridge. A cloud slid across the sun and the air cooled a little more.

"I ain't planning on killing nobody on my own front porch," Beanpole said. "I wouldn't do my wife that way."

"Then how about you take that gun you got and put it on the table."

"Can you see it?"

"No, but it's there, ain't it."

Beanpole removed the Colt revolver from a deep pocket and placed it on his wife's tin-topped table, barrel aimed at the woods.

"I seen a man get beat to death with a ball-peen hammer," he said. "You want me to throw my tools in the creek, too?"

"I don't see no hammer."

Tucker climbed the steps and sat in a wooden chair. He slouched to access his pistol, the back rail pressing into his shoulder blades. Beanpole eased into the other chair.

"You satisfied?" Beanpole said.

"No," Tucker said. "You made a mistake."

"I made maybe a thousand."

"You give your pistol up too quick. That means you got another gun handy. My opinion it's a shotgun right inside that door."

"Could be a belly gun."

"I seen a man carry one of them two-shot derringers hanging on a string inside his shirt. They ain't got a safety. Old boy shot hisself in the peter."

"Shoot it off or just a little nick?"

"I never asked."

"I ain't packing no belly gun," Beanpole said.

"I don't reckon you could get at it if you had one. You'd get shot three or four times before you could dig it out."

"That a joke?"

"Yup."

"Not funny."

"Nope. They a shotgun in that doorway?"

"Yup."

Tucker lit a Lucky. He'd worked for Beanpole longer than any of the other drivers. Tucker knew all the routes, drop-offs and pick-ups, the patrol schedule of bent lawmen, where to hide, what doctor and mechanic to turn to, and everybody's names. He could send Beanpole to prison. Every day Tucker walked the earth made him more of a threat. He suddenly thought of something else—maybe Beanpole got trapped by the Feds and this whole porch visit was an elaborate ruse to turn him in.

"You working with the tax agents?" he said.

"Hell, no," Beanpole said.

"Then what is it you're wanting?"

"You and me, we got us a problem. Two of them."

Tucker pinched the fire off the cigarette end, bent it in half, and tucked it in his pocket. Later he'd transfer it to a coffee can full of old butts for emergency use when he ran out of store-bought and had to roll his own. He shifted his body, moving his hand closer to the pistol. Tucker didn't have any problems and didn't know what Beanpole was talking about.

"Thing is," Beanpole said, "you know I got that bootlegger."

"On the county line."

"Beer. Half pints of government whiskey. Pints of wine."

"Wyatt still running it?"

"Yes, he does. Steady money, regular as Little Liver pills. Not like shine which is up and down and all over the place."

"You ain't had no problem with me."

"You're the best I got," Beanpole said. "I mean the money itself is up and down. I don't know from week to week how much liquor them stillers will make. They spill it or bust the jars. Sometimes they drink it up and shoot each other."

"I know it. Had them to not show up for a load more than once."

"That's right. Many's the time you had to fool around up in Ohio waiting on getting paid or getting your car worked on or something."

"I ain't never fooled around."

"Didn't mean it that way, Tucker. What I'm trying to say, I don't always know how much or when the shine money's coming. May as well say which way a bird'll fly off a fence. Then there's gasoline which ain't getting cheaper. Sugar, cornmeal, yeast, malt. Payoffs to all and sundry. Helping out men to keep them working—take care of somebody's doctor bill or put school clothes on a man's kids. I got to give money to every politician and preacher in six counties. You want to know how I got this fat? All I do is visit folks to keep business going smooth, and every time I see somebody I got to set down and eat with them. They's times I ate four or five full meals a day."

Tucker nodded. He'd never heard Beanpole go on this way, and figured he was building up to something. His body relaxed a little. Whatever Beanpole had in mind, it wasn't shooting Tucker. Maybe he just needed to run his mouth. He'd known men to do that, like opening a valve, but Beanpole never made any kind of move without plenty of forethought. Tucker smoked and waited.

"What I'm getting at," Beanpole said, "is the bootlegger income is all I got for reliable. I know exactly what the cost is and how much I'll get back. That's the money behind everything else. Like motor oil in an engine. And the engine runs it all."

"I'd say it's more like gas."

"What?"

"The bootlegger money you're bragging on is the fuel, not the grease."

"You're right," Beanpole said. "Damned if you ain't. And that's the problem. I got to keep that bootlegger up or the whole thing will fall apart. It finances the whole kit and kaboodle."

"Ain't got nothing to do with me," Tucker said.

"I know that. I damn sure do. You ain't stole no cash. People get along with you. You handle yourself good when things get out of hand. And you ain't never spent one night in jail. Right?"

Tucker nodded.

"I know around here, no," Beanpole said. "But I ain't for sure about up in Ohio and Michigan. Could be you got locked up and kept it to yourself."

"Nope."

"Or before. When you was in the service?"

"They didn't have no jail where I was at in Korea. What in the hell are you getting at? I'm tired of waiting and listening to you crying."

Beanpole tipped his rocker forward, the wood creaking. A stray poplar leaf, already brittle and yellow, blew across the yard. The dogs were a distant din. Initial conversation had gone well—he had Tucker's attention, which was the goal. Beanpole liked him personally and respected the hardships of his life. All those messed-up kids offered cover and plenty of built-in sympathy. Rhonda was as good a runner's wife as any—closemouthed, tough as hickory, and loyal to the bone.

"My problem," Beanpole said, "is this. Every two or three years, some politician gets a wild hare up his ass and sets about making it rough on bootleggers. Now it's my turn in the barrel."

"County or state?"

"State this time. A lawyer fixing to run for office. Trying to make a name for hisself."

"I thought you bribed all them bastards off."

"He's a young feller. I can't buy him till he gets elected. He shuts down my bootlegger, he shuts down all of us—you and everybody else."

"Close up a couple of weeks," Tucker said. "You done that before."

"That's the plan all right. But this lawyer, he wants a big show to get his picture in the papers."

"All them dumb-asses want that."

"He's aiming to raid it. A buddy in the state police told me the exact day and time. They'll put the man on trial and send him away."

"Wyatt?"

"No, it can't be Wyatt. He's done went twice. They'll keep his ass till he's dead. I got to put another man in Wyatt's place when the raid comes."

"Well," Tucker said, "there's Joe-Eddie."

"You didn't hear?"

"Hear what?"

"Joe-Eddie's setting in the Mount Sterling jailhouse over some kind of shoot-out with three men."

"Three?"

"He was mixed up with a woman and shot her husband first. Then the husband's brother. And the brother-in-law."

"Any hurt bad?"

"No, didn't kill a one, but he damn sure never let up on them. He won't get out of jail till after the raid."

"Why not?"

"He shot that whole damn family up," Beanpole said. "They're keeping him in to protect him. They done arrested one brother and two cousins trying to shoot him through the jail windows."

"Ol' Joe-Eddie. He's all right when he's asleep."

Tucker grinned and they chuckled together, watching a wasp crawl headfirst down a porch post. Beanpole shifted the rocker and lifted his boot and the wasp flew east straight as a rope.

"Old boy up to Ohio," Tucker said, "told me something might work for you. Said he put a woman up on a raid to get arrested. She wore a nice dress to court, had her hair and nails did. The judge liked her. Time served, a fine, and out the door she went."

"Not a bad idea. You got a woman in mind?"

Tucker fired up a cigarette. He saw in his mind a map of the main road and the creek, ridges and hollers, and all the houses. He examined each family in turn, counting the potential women likely to go along with getting paid for jail. Most were unsuitable—too churchy or had kids. Some were too old and others too young. About a quarter were married to men with criminal records.

"My opinion," Tucker said, "they ain't nobody but them three Branham sisters, live up Lick Fork."

"Oldest got married here lately."

"Candy? Who'd marry her?"

"I don't know," Beanpole said. "I don't even know which one it was."

"Candy's got them ears goes to a point, and black-headed."

"Yeah, that's the one got married. Might have moved to Elliott County."

"There's Gloria," Tucker said.

"She can't count her titties twice and come up with the same number."

"That'll make the law go easy."

"Maybe so. But she won't be able to keep her story straight. She'll mess it up every time she tells it till she lets out the whole deal."

"That leaves Loretta. I know her, she's the smartest of the bunch."

"No," Beanpole said. "Something's wrong with her."

"Like what?"

"Brain attack, my wife thinks," Beanpole said. "Can't hardly get around. Talking funny. Drooling. Part of her face don't work right. Ain't no judge will believe she was bootlegging."

Tucker could see where this was headed and didn't like it. The more worthless gibble-gabble they did, the more time he had to prepare a response to what was coming. Tucker was the only man working for Beanpole who hadn't been arrested, and now it appeared to be a liability.

"You said they was two problems," Tucker said.

"Yep. This here's mine. The other's yours."

"I don't reckon."

"Few months back a man got killed over in Salt Lick."

"Joe-Eddie again?"

"No. Somebody stabbed a man in front of that diner with the windows."

"Didn't hear nothing on it," Tucker said.

"He's some kind of bigwig in Frankfort. They got the law all over it."

"Still yet, they do?"

"They quit for a while," Beanpole said. "But they're back on it. State police now."

"Why's that?"

"Somebody seen a car."

"Did they?"

"Listen a minute, Tucker. I got me a pet cop over there. The car they're talking about sounds a lot like your run-car. Now my cop, he made sure and didn't put that down on any report he turned in back when it happened. But the state boys, they went around talking to everybody again. The same man, he told them about the car. This time they got paperwork on it. They're hunting that car and pretty soon they'll find it."

"A man seen my car over there?"

"That's what they're saying, yes."

"Not a woman, but a man."

"No, not no woman."

"Pay him off," Tucker said.

"Done tried. This feller, he's a deacon and a Democrat. His wife's got some kind of sick dog needs walking on a leash every night. He seen the car. Color, make, model, and county plate. All a match to yours."

Tucker stopped rocking, stopped looking at the woods and the sky, stopped hearing the dogs. It wasn't the woman who was talking and that was good. But the rest of it wasn't any good. Tucker could threaten the man but that might make it worse. No telling what kind of son-of-a-bitch went out of the evening with a dog on a rope.

"I ain't saying you done it," Beanpole said. "Nobody is. But right now they're hunting that car."

"Reckon they are."

"They ain't no easy path to chop out here, Tuck."

"Ain't that always the way of it."

"My wife says the good Lord laid out a rough road for all of us, and we just got to take it and keep taking it and it'll get better one of these days."

"Uh-huh. One of these days ain't coming fast enough."

"Sometimes we got to help things along. I don't mean help the Lord, you understand. I mean just lay out a route down that rough road He put in front of us."

"Us?" Tucker said. "I ain't heard nothing about no us. I heard a bunch of horseshit about a raid, and a bigger bunch of horseshit about a car. They's a lot of cars in the world."

"You're right. New cars every day. Half the boys around here are moving up to Detroit to build them. But not that many cars are mixed up with a killing and running shine. And setting in front of your house with everybody knowing who drives it and who he drives for."

Tucker pondered Beanpole's words. The car made him vulnerable and put his family at risk. He didn't mind getting arrested but not in front of his wife and kids.

"I'll get rid of the car," Tucker said.

"How? You can't sell it or trade it. The paper'll run right back up your backside and you still yet owned it when that man got killed."

"I'll figure something out."

"I already did."

"I ain't going to prison for you."

Tucker shifted in his chair, placing the full force of his gaze on Beanpole's face. Hidden by his leg, he flexed his fingers. If Beanpole intended violence, now would be the time.

"Listen," Beanpole said. "Just hear the idea. You've knowed me a long time. I ain't had a plan yet go sideways on me. If you don't like what I say, we'll pick at it like crows. All right?"

"I'll listen," Tucker said. "But I ain't going to prison."

"You want anything to drink?"

"No, damn it, I don't drink. And I don't want you going inside where that shotgun's at. So get your damn talking done. Then I'll go to the house because I damn sure ain't going to the pen for you."

Tucker slouched and twisted until he was lying in the chair at an angle, his backside barely on the edge of the seat, his legs straight. His hand was two inches from his revolver.

Beanpole knew that Tucker could draw and shoot faster than taking a breath. He was either-handed as a spider and had a knife somewhere on him, too. Beanpole tipped his head and talked to the ceiling, his voice slow, putting as much soothing emphasis as he could on each word.

"Say a man was to take over that little bootlegger shack for while. Say that man got picked up in a raid. Why, there'd be all manner of customer to say that same man had been bootlegging there for a year. No way he was in Salt Lick on such-and-such a night. They'd swear it on a stack of Bibles because that's what they'd get paid to tell. Say that man goes to court. He's a good man, a family man, never been in no trouble, a decorated veteran. Say he's got young kids to provide for. Because of them, he can't go north for no factory job.

"This man has a lawyer that lines all this out. The judge gives him easy time, six or eight months. While he's inside, the man's wife gets twenty-five dollars a week. Enough to pay all the bills, the bank loan on the land, ever what the kids need extra. Say on top of that the man's wife has a car give to her. She needs that car because the other one is gone, nobody knows where to, but it is gone for good. The man does his time and comes home. The day he gets out, he gets a bonus of two thousand dollars cash.

"This man, he's in better shape than he is right now. The police are looking for a car that ain't around no more. And the man's got an alibi for Salt Lick. He ain't got nothing to worry about. His family's took care of and a pot of money is waiting on him."

Beanpole's neck was sore from staring straight up but he didn't move. He could feel waves of tension emanating from Tucker like ripples around a tree stump snagged in a river.

"I can't go to prison," Tucker said.

"Nobody wants to."

"I mean, I can't."

"Why not?"

"Rhonda's pregnant."

"Uh-huh," Beanpole said. "I see how that puts a stopper in things."

He stared into the tree line, pretending to think it over. His wife had already told him Rhonda was expecting, and Beanpole had figured out how to use the information to his advantage. He'd long ago learned that the best way to win people over was do them a favor ahead of time. The tricky part was learning what that favor was. In Tucker's case, it was simple.

"When's the baby due?" Beanpole said.

"Three weeks."

"Well then," Beanpole said. "What in case I make sure that raid don't happen till after the baby's born."

"You can do that?"

Beanpole nodded. There was no designated time. He'd lied to make Tucker feel beholden to him.

"Yes, I can do that," he said. He rubbed the back of his head. "My neck fat aches from looking up."

"What about the car?"

"What about it?"

"What's your big plan to get rid of it?" Tucker said.

"Run it in the Number Nine mine. It's the last one they built so it's the widest. The first tunnel ends at one big drop-off. You can throw a rock in and not hear it hit."

"Reckon a car would fit?"

"Might scrape the sides," Beanpole said, "but it'll make it."

"It's a damn good car."

"I don't see no other way."

Tucker had drawn his body back into the chair and was sitting normally, hands resting on his thighs. It wasn't a bad idea. He'd have a record, but that didn't matter in the hills, especially for selling beer to drunks. Going to prison was a possibility he'd accepted on his first run, same as getting killed.

"I don't want nobody bothering Rhonda and the kids with me gone."

"It won't be easy."

"Setting in a cell ain't easy."

"All right," Beanpole said. "I'll move them. That way if anybody comes around, Rhonda and the kids won't be there."

"Where to?"

"Here," Beanpole said. "My road ain't on any map. Rhonda'll be all right up here."

"Your wife won't like that."

"I don't mean living with us. Angela's off with the grandkids half the time. She's been on me about moving closer to them."

"I ain't renting off you."

"What we do is buy each other's house for one dollar. Put it in your wife's family name."

"Might work," Tucker said. "But twenty-five dollars a week in prison won't cut it. I want sixty a week. Plus fifteen thousand cash when I get out."

Beanpole massaged his neck with his fingers, straining his arm to reach. He relaxed a little. Now that Tucker was haggling, the deal was as good as done. He'd been wondering how much Tucker would ask for. He admired him for going full on.

"Can't do it," Beanpole said. "Ain't got it."

"I know how much you make off me and how many runners you got. A minute ago you set right there bragging about the bootlegger money."

"I won't be making no money off you."

"I won't be making none setting in a cell."

Beanpole enjoyed negotiation, but it was always more fun with someone who liked it, too. He knew Tucker wasn't that way.

"Forty a week and ten thousand when you get out," Beanpole said.

Languidly at first and then in a quick motion, Tucker pushed himself from the chair and offered his hand.

"Forty a week," Tucker said. "And ten thousand."

Beanpole rose and stuck his own meaty hand out. They shook once, then dropped their arms. Tucker left the porch, his back to Beanpole for the first time, a shoulder twitching where he felt an imaginary bullet strike. He stopped and looked at the land, turning in a slow circle to the porch. The house was bigger than his and in better shape, and the driveway was gravel.

"Hey," he said to Beanpole. "You best go to the doctors about that neck fat."

Tucker waved and drove away. At the foot of his home hill he parked by the creek and smoked a cigarette. He couldn't decide what to tell Rhonda first—the new house or him going away for a while. They hadn't been getting along since he got in from his last run. He wanted a warm welcome home but she always felt overwhelmed and irritable. She was worried that the next baby would be a boy not quite right in the head. Maybe the promise of money would help. He plucked a double handful of purple birdsfoot and white crownbeard, laid them on the truck seat, and drove home.

Chapter Eight

A few days later, Tucker walked through the woods at dusk and climbed the hill. Lightning bugs flickered low. He'd heard the females were the ones that lit up in order to attract males, which made sense for a bug that only went out at night. Hills ran at a steep slant on either side of the creek, blocking starlight. Tucker didn't mind. He'd walked here many times as a kid.

He shifted the ruck across his shoulders. The load wasn't too heavy but he'd lost the habit of wearing it, and the calluses along his collarbones had softened. Discomfort turned to nagging pain that he ignored like a chigger bite. He was glad to be born and raised on a ridge where people got more daylight. Families who lived up narrow hollers only saw solid sun three or four hours per day. They were a pale bunch. If you were going to make a home in a holler, you may as well live in town, and if you did that, why not go whole hog and move to Lexington.

At the top of the hill Tucker found the entrance to Number Nine. The narrow gauge railway was gone, but a few rotted ties still protruded from the earth. He pulled a flashlight from his ruck and stepped into the mine. Old beer cans and cigarette butts littered the first fifteen feet. His boots were loud in the silence. The shaft narrowed at a slight turn and he measured the width to make sure his car would fit. Farther on, the shaft made a fork and the old rail line veered to the left. Tucker moved carefully along the right fork, sliding his boots a few inches at a time.

The air ahead became darker. He scooped a handful of rock and threw it past the flashlight's beam. When it struck the earth, he moved a few feet more, and did it again. There was no sound. He knelt and crawled, moving his fingers along the surface. Finding the edge of the drop-off sent a jolt through him as if he'd grabbed a live electrical wire. He tossed a rock into the abyss and heard nothing. The miners had inadvertently found a pit cave, a natural vertical shaft that ended in a cavern far below. Tucker underwent a strange impulse to lean forward and fall, as if the deep cavity in the earth were beckoning.

He set the flashlight on the ground. From the ruck he withdrew a hammer, an old T-shirt, and a sharpened picket of oak. He pounded the picket into the dirt six inches from the edge of the hole. Satisfied that it was firmly in place, he draped the white T-shirt over the top. Tucker walked back out of the mine and descended the hill. The moon had risen. The woods had encroached upon the narrow road but rain kept it washed out. It was rough in places, more creek than road. The run-car would make it easily, the gears and suspension modified for traction.

At the house he watched Big Billy sleep. Rhonda rose and went to the bathroom, nodding to him in a blur of somnolence, and he heard the bedsprings creak as she returned to sleep. She'd been upset since learning about the deal he'd made with Beanpole. Tucker had repeatedly emphasized the new house—more rooms, better insulation, warmer in winter. He impressed upon her the amount of money they'd receive in less than a year. She wanted to know why—why him, why now, why why why? He explained that serving a little prison time was part of his job.

He slept in a chair until dawn, then moved to the bed for an hour. He rose for coffee with Rhonda on the porch. He lit a Lucky and waited for her to speak. Jo brought them yesterday's biscuits with ham, then went back inside. Tucker heard her climbing the steps and singing to her siblings.

"She's a good girl," he said.

Rhonda nodded.

"Helps with the little ones," he said.

Rhonda stared at the yard as if something existed other than fescue. Her hair hung lank and uncombed. Despite sitting in a rocking chair, she was motionless.

"Rhonda," he said, but didn't know how to go on. "Rhonda . . . Think it'll rain?"

She nodded.

"Frog strangler," he said, "gully-warsher, or a cow pissing through a screen door?"

"Light," she whispered. "Dry again by evening."

"Did you ever want an umbrella? They got them in town. I never seen nobody use one but they might be handy."

"No," she said. "Won't help in a flood."

"Can't flood a hill."

"It's what it's like."

"What?"

"You gone six months. This baby coming. Like the world is drowning and me with it."

"I'll be back before that baby's walking and we'll have ten thousand dollars cash and a bigger house."

"I'd rather have you."

"You do, Rhonda. You got me right here."

He didn't understand her talk of drowning. He'd grown up with sisters and a mother, but the ways of women were a mystery. By age eight, boys in the hills spent all their time outside while women stayed indoors unless they were gardening or killing a chicken. Maybe that's why women lived longer. Or maybe he had it backwards and men lived shorter.

"I had me a dream last night," Rhonda said.

"A dream."

"I was in an airplane. It didn't have no roof on it. Just open to the sky. The driver of it was sitting behind me. Beside me was our new baby, a boy. The sky was pretty. All them clouds. I started in looking for you on the ground but couldn't see you. Everybody else I ever knowed was there, even some that's been dead for many a year. But not you."

She trailed off. Tucker had been in the middle of lighting a cigarette and stopped. He figured dreams didn't amount to much but people always wanted their own to mean something.

"Don't sound like too bad a dream to me," he said.

"No," she said. "I liked it. Flying in a plane. I never seen one and there I was in one. It was nice."

"And the boy was there."

She nodded.

"Did he have a name?" he said.

"I don't want to name him yet, in case he ain't right."

"Will that make a difference? The name?"

"If something's wrong with him, I want to save the good name for the next baby."

Tucker nodded. Two red squirrels chased each other around an oak at the edge of the yard, then ran up the tree. At the first fork the small one went east. The other squirrel jumped to the opposite fork and they faced each other on a long horizontal limb. The big one jumped the other, landing easily on the bark, spinning on its rear legs. It climbed on the back of the small one, tucked its forelegs tight, and began hunching its tiny hips. In a few weeks the squirrel would give birth, same as Rhonda. The male might be shot by then, same as him.

Tucker stood and went into the house and got his gun and returned to the porch. She glanced at the pistol he'd brought out.

"Just old habit," he said. "From the army."

"You never once told me anything about over there."

"Not much to say, Rhonda. Me and my brothers used to play army in the woods. It was the same. Except not so many trees and the guns were real."

"You mean it was fun?"

"No."

"You used to have bad dreams about it," she said.

"That's why I don't put much stock in dreams. I decided I'd not remember them and they went away."

"I liked flying. But I didn't know where you were at. It made me nervous."

"Well," he said, "pretty soon you'll know exactly where I'm at for six months. You'll be way ahead of all the other women worried their men are out catting around."

Rhonda's eyes squinted with a slight smile. Her shoulders rose and fell, the laughter unable to leave her body. Tucker put his hand over hers. At his touch, she began to cry. He stood and leaned over her for a hug. The chair arms got in his way and she couldn't scoot forward because of her belly, nine months swollen. He knelt on the porch slats and laid his head against her. His strong arms circled her waist.

They sat that way for a long time, days it seemed to Rhonda. She looked at the top of his head and knew she'd found him from the plane. He was here. He'd go away but come back. Six months was short. He'd be back before the baby was walking. She felt a sudden cramp deep in her body, an involuntary flexing. Her time was coming soon, a couple of days or so.

Tucker spent an hour with the girls in the upstairs bedroom and two hours talking to Billy. As Rhonda foretold, the early afternoon received a light rain that turned every surface into a prism. The woods glowed in the sun. He took Jo on a walk, showing her where mistletoe grew in the bare branches of blackgum, explaining that her mother would appreciate some at Christmas.

"I want some dryland fish," she said. "Are they biting yet?"

"No, Jo. They ain't exactly fish, but a kind of mushroom."

"Why do they call it a fish?"

"You take and cut one in half and it looks like a fish."

She laughed, the sound drifting up the holler to mingle with the early doves.

"They's some to call it a hickory chicken," he said. "I don't know why."

"I'm going to call them a chicken-fish."

"Good idea. Then nobody will know what you're talking about."

"Why's that good?" she said.

"If you ain't careful somebody'll follow you and take all your fish. They grow in patches and you don't want nobody knowing where they're at."

"Will you show me?"

"They don't grow the same place every year. You got to wait till oak leaves are the size of a mouse ear, then go look for mayapples, before they flower. They favor the hillsides on the north. Some sun but not too much. Right about the time sarvis is blooming, look under oak and beech. You find one, you stop right there and look around in circles."

"They grow in circles?"

"If you throw a rock in a mud hole, the water makes circles. That's how you hunt dryland fish. You look for the rings from the first one you find."

He stopped walking and looked at her, waiting.

"Mouse ear and oak," she said. "Sarvis and mayapple. Mud hole circles. Which way's north?"

"Moss grows on the north side of trees."

"How does a tree have sides if it's round-shaped?"

"I don't know. That's about the smartest thing I heard anybody say."

He watched her preen beneath the praise. They stopped at a flat place on the hill, a mini-ridge that overlooked the holler. He sat on a damp rock protruding half a foot from the earth.

"This is my spot, Jo. I moved this rock up here when I was about your age. You need to study on something alone, you come here to this spot. If I ain't around, you can talk to me here."

"Can I sit on your rock?"

"All you want. It's colder than the dirt. But dries faster after rain."

Jo propped her elbows on his thigh and looked around, memorizing the place and the route. Time spent with her father was rare. This was the most she could ever remember him talking except late at night to Big Billy.

"Honey," he said. "Your mama'll have a new baby soon. And I'll be gone for a while. She'll need you more than ever."

"Where are you going? Can I come?"

"No, you can't. It's not for kids."

"I don't want you to go, Daddy."

"I don't either. Neither does Mommy. But it's the way of it."

"Why?"

"Comes a time," he said and stopped. "A man . . ."

He trailed away and reached involuntarily to light a Lucky, but decided against it because her face was close to his.

"Jo. I just got to go. It's sort of like work. Except longer. That's about all there is to say. But I'll be back."

She nodded. As long as Jo could remember, her father had come and gone at indeterminate hours for various lengths of time. He always brought back something nice, just for her. She knew kids at school who had no father, and others whose father never worked. She believed she had the best daddy of all. They walked down the hill together. Jo felt lighter now, unburdened without knowing she'd previously carried a load. In the coming months she figured she'd go up to her daddy's spot once a week, maybe take a broom and sweep it clean for his return.

Tucker rested for a couple of hours, a state not quite sleep, a skill he'd learned in the army. He could relax his body but come fully alert in less than a second. He rose for a meal of soup beans, cornbread, and collard greens. He cleared out the car and unscrewed the side mirrors. He circled it once, brushing his fingers over two bullet holes he'd carefully repaired. He loaded the trunk with a tractor jack, a hickory post, a blanket, a hatchet, a sledgehammer, a flashlight, and rope.

He turned the key, enjoying the low rumble as he eased out the ridge to a fire trail and followed the old mine road. He was tired. Maybe prison would be a good break. The constant vigilance drained him, the steady threat of robbery or arrest. Living on coffee, potted ham, and crackers had cost his guts. He couldn't tally the number of times he'd slept in the car holding a pistol. Tucker was lucky—he'd never been caught and he'd lost only one vehicle, abandoning it in a pond and escaping on foot. He'd bought the old Ford coupe and set about modifying it. The years of running had been fun but he was done for a while.

At the entrance to the mine he cut the engine and stepped into the woods, listening intently for twenty minutes. Either nobody had followed him or someone was laying back a long ways. He cut six long boughs of pine, each with smaller limbs forking away, and tied the limbs to the rear bumper. The tasseled pine needles dragged the ground behind the tires, erasing tracks.

Tucker broke the rear window with the sledgehammer and draped the blanket over the jagged edge of the opening. He turned on the headlights and drove slowly into the mine. The space ahead was illuminated for a few feet before the darkness seemed to suck the light away. The left side of the car scraped the wall. He maintained a steady pace, slow as possible to keep from stalling. The shaft tightened at a slight turn, the rock tearing a gash in the Ford's body. He kept his boots on both the accelerator and clutch pedal, lifting and pushing each until the car was past the gouging rock. The passage forked left and he steered the opposite way and saw the white T-shirt hanging on the oak picket. He shifted into neutral, climbed into the backseat, and crawled out through the broken rear window. The shaft was silent, the air completely black. He removed his tools from the trunk.

He squatted with his back against the bumper and pushed. His leg muscles quivered from the effort. He'd pushed it before but that had been on blacktop with less friction. Now he strained with every part of himself. The car began rolling forward and he felt the abrupt shift as the front wheels dropped over the edge. They landed hard.

He placed the tractor jack beneath the rear of the car, then set the post horizontally on the jack. He began operating the handle. The car rose slowly, the hickory post distributing the weight. When the rear tires were clear of the earth, he pushed the car until it fell forward off the jack, moving farther into the hole. Tucker repeated this process several times until the car tipped completely over the edge. Tucker heard it hit an outcrop, then twenty seconds later a dull impact. A few pine needles lay at the lip of the abyss. He threw them into the hole along with the jack, post, and T-shirt.

He knew he was vulnerable now, cornered with one way out. Killing him would solve all Beanpole's problems, plus save money. Tucker turned off the flashlight and walked through the black air, his left hand touching the wall for guidance. The car's passage had stirred dust that was still settling. He felt it in his eyes and nose and throat. He sipped water. The heavy darkness softened and he withdrew his pistol. He pressed his back to the wall and sidled forward, staying inside the shadow. The opening was dark gray in the blackness. He stopped and listened and heard nothing. He moved forward, leading with his gun. He watched the trees lining the road, seeking a flash of moonlight on metal, an unnatural form, anything out of place. Satisfied that he was alone, he stepped furtively from the mine and began the long walk home. He felt a vague relief but maintained his vigilance.

Two hours later he circled his house twice, staying inside the perimeter of woods, rousing nothing but dogs. He sat on the porch and lit a cigarette. His body was worn down to a nub, but his mind was quick, his thoughts rampant. He'd not heard an explosion but the car could have caught fire after he left. Smoke would wend through the chambers of the cave and interlocking mine shafts, making the source difficult to trace. Smoke might rise from a hole two miles from the mine. Tucker finished his cigarette and went to bed.

Four days later Rhonda gave birth to a boy, alert and squally. His hair was so white and thin that his scalp gleamed and Tucker called him "Shiny." As soon as Rhonda was able, he moved the family and his small amount of possessions to the new house purchased for a dollar from Beanpole. Jo had her own room and the little ones had theirs. An extra room would serve for the boy when he got older.

The week before Tucker was slated to work the bootlegger shack, he ate as much as possible. His only culinary skill was breakfast, which he prepared four times a day, improving slightly on the biscuits. He held his infant son. No matter which way Tucker moved his head, the boy's eyes followed him. His fingers clutched tight as bark to a tree. He stared at light and seemed to know the sound of his mother's voice. Tucker felt gratitude of a previously unknown depth. Rhonda cried once, but it went on for hours, as if she was shedding every speck of sorrow she'd ever felt. Afterward she was lighthearted as a kitten. She and Tucker sat with Jo in the kitchen.

"We need to name that boy," Rhonda said. "Shiny ain't enough for that little feller."

"You got a name in mind?" Tucker said.

"After his daddy."

"No, I don't hold with Juniors. I've knowed four and never liked them."

"He's a boy so it ort to be a name in your family. The girls got mine."

"I know it," he said. "But let's start a new name."

"A new name, Daddy?" Jo said.

"Maybe Cornbread," he said. "How about Mailbox?"

"They're not names." She frowned and looked at Rhonda. "Are they, Mommy?"

"No, your daddy's funning with you. He means a name ain't got used by the family yet."

"Randall," he said. "Randall something Tucker. You-uns pick out the middle part. Maybe Goat or Sycamore or something."

"Ryan," Rhonda said. "Randy Ryan."

"Little Randy Ryan," Jo said.

Tucker nodded. The baby wanted to nurse and Tucker went outside. He sat on the porch, trying to memorize the contour of the trees against the night. He was tired of running shine and this was a good solution. Six months, then ten thousand dollars. Maybe he'd open a little general store, teach his son to help. The boy was normal, anybody could see that.

The next day he dismantled his revolver, oiled the pieces, wrapped them in greased cloth, and put them in a sack. He pried a board free inside a closet and drove two nails into a stud. On them he hung the sack and his sheathed Ka-Bar knife. He carefully refastened the board.

In the late afternoon he carried each of his young children to the table and they ate together. Afterward he returned them to their rooms. He and Rhonda lay in their bed with the baby between them. They didn't talk. At dusk he rose and kissed each child, then returned to his bedroom. He sat on the edge of the bed and took Rhonda's hand.

"Keep them babies warm," he said.

"Come back," she said.

He nodded and left the house unarmed for the first time he could remember. The bootlegger was three miles away by road, or one mile through the woods. He climbed the steep slope to his spot, scuffed aside the damp leaves, and sat on the flat rock. Sound interlaced through the woods—dove, owl, whip-poor-will, the cough of a deer, the rustle of raccoon and possum. He looked at the few stars visible between treetops. They'd be here when he returned, along with his spot and his family.

He rose and followed a rain gully to a creek, crossed the road, and climbed the next hill. He walked the ridge until he was above the bootlegger, then descended. From the building protruded a rough wood shelf topped with a sliding panel. He rapped on it twice and the panel opened. The man jerked his head and Tucker walked behind the shack. A door opened and the man left quickly on foot. Tucker stepped inside. A bare bulb hung from a rafter. The ceiling and two walls facing wind were insulated. Three game freezers held beer. Several boxes contained half pints of whiskey and fifths of wine. Suspended on a pair of hooks below the paneled window was a sawed-off shotgun. Tucker unloaded it and sat in a chair. On a plank table were an ashtray, a cigar box full of money, and extra shells for the shotgun. One corner held a five-gallon bucket and a roll of toilet paper.

No customers arrived, the word having gone out that the raid would occur. Tucker smoked. Three hours passed. He heard car engines outside. Red light flashed through cracks in the wall. He opened the wood panel to a pair of policeman, who told Tucker to go out the back, where two more policemen stood. Tucker underwent arrest without incident and they drove him to the Morehead jail, built from the same brown granite as his old grade school. The jailer knew him and treated him well—plenty of food, coffee, and cigarettes. On a chilly night Tucker received an extra blanket.

A week later he stood trial. His lawyer said he'd worked at the bootlegger for a year, had no previous record, and was a decorated veteran. The judge sentenced him to eight months in a state correctional facility.

Chapter Nine

Tucker began his sentence at La Grange, a minimum-security penitentiary that operated as a work farm on a thousand acres. Initially he didn't know what to do. Many cons slept. They called it "fast time" because it eradicated the hours as if they had never existed. Within a month he settled into the routines of labor, meals, and sleep. He smoked less. Daily exercise returned his body to a muscled state that years of driving had taken away. The structure of prison reminded him of army life—it provided him with clothes, food, a bed, and the constant company of men. His cellmate had been in state and federal prisons and claimed the only difference was the quality of female visitors. Federal institutions had better-looking women. Tucker took his word for it, hoping he'd never learn if it was true or not.

Most inmates were veterans of Korea and World War II, trained for violence but not in how to control it. Tucker knew he didn't fall into that category. Half were crazy as a soup sandwich and the rest were dumb as dirt. None had ever had two nickels to rub together and all of them blamed someone for their incarceration—a woman, a partner, a snitch, or a cop. Getting locked down was a choice Tucker had made, a fact he never told anyone. He didn't think in terms of innocence and guilt, good and bad, or whether he deserved to be there. He regretted nothing and blamed no one. He was getting paid.

On a cloudy Saturday during rec time in the yard, a long skinny shard of sunshine slid across the dirt and rose along a concrete wall. Tucker traced the light's progress in advance and positioned himself where the sun would arrive, waiting for the heat against his face. A scrawny man with a dark beard stepped in front of Tucker, blocking the light, then tried to jostle him aside. Tucker held his ground. After a brief confrontation, he shoved the man, who retaliated with a long looping right hook. Tucker leaned in and punched the man in the throat. He staggered to his knees. The shrill sound of guard whistles cut the air, scattering the inmates.

A day later, the bearded man attacked Tucker in the chow line, slashing his shoulder with a homemade knife. Tucker deftly took the weapon, broke the man's arm, and sat down to eat. The guards hadn't seen the quick scuffle and Tucker denied that anything had happened. The man was a member of the Dayton Satans, an Ohio motorcycle club with three men incarcerated at La Grange. The other two bikers approached Tucker and explained that one of Beanpole's corrupt cops had testified against them, and Tucker was a target of vengeance. The attacks would end if he agreed to move contraband within the prison. He refused.

A blitz attack could come any time but Tucker figured the bikers would wait until Monday, when they were on work detail. He'd seen fights behind the toolhouse. If a brawl didn't erupt, the guards let the men fight, hoping both prisoners would be out of circulation for a while. Tucker kept the weapon he'd taken from the biker under his mattress. It was the footrest of a shovel, four inches long, honed on one side. The end was squared and blunt like a straight razor. Medical tape wrapped the other end. He spent three hours bending the metal tip—first one way, then the other—using as a fulcrum a bolt that fastened his bunk to the floor. The bent metal finally snapped at an angle. His hands were sore and his knuckles bled from scraping cement but he had a tapered blade good for stabbing.

At meals Tucker made sure to eat near the guards, refusing to shower or spend rec time with the other men, who steered clear of him, knowing he was marked. The Satans called him chicken and yellow and punk, but he ignored their scorn. He intended to fight on his terms. If they believed he was ducking them, they'd come when he gave them the opportunity. On Sunday after chapel, he traded all his cigarettes for magazines with lurid covers featuring a woman in a torn dress. The pages were printed on wood pulp paper. Originally a half inch thick, they'd been passed from cell to cell long enough to lose their bulk, some pages torn out and saved for their imagery, others stuck together and removed in disgust.

Rising early on Monday morning, Tucker used the makeshift blade to cut his sheet into long strips, which he wrapped around his waist, tying the ends in a slipknot. He slid a magazine between the sheet and his stomach, then ran a row around his torso, overlapping them like shingles. Satisfied with their placement, he cinched the slipknot tight. He strapped two magazines to each forearm, spines facing out. His prison-issue clothes fit loose enough to hide the makeshift armor as long as he didn't bend his body too much in any direction. The weapon fit easily up his sleeve, lodged within the pages. He removed his socks before lacing his shoes. He'd get blisters, but if blood ran down his legs, it would fill his shoes before spilling out. He'd seen men lose their lives slipping in blood on the ground.

He ate breakfast sitting at an awkward angle to prevent the magazines from pushing against his clothes and alerting the guards. As the men left mess and headed through the doors to work in a field, Tucker made sure he was near the front of the line. Morning sun was burning away shoals of ground fog in the distance. The cons were mostly silent, feeling a generalized tension, aware of the impending violence. They walked quickly against the chill, bunched up in line at the toolhouse.

Tucker turned around and looked for the two bikers, who stared mad-dog eyes, the bigger one drawing a forefinger across his throat in warning.

"Hey," Tucker said, "if you feel froggy, come around here and jump."

He stepped behind the toolhouse and stood several feet from the wall to give himself room to maneuver. The winner of a knife fight was the man who bled to death slowest. The big man came first, wielding a wooden clothes hanger studded on both sides with embedded razors. He swung it in a figure eight. The man had long arms, but could only slash, not stab. Tucker stepped forward and hopped back, circling to his right, as the man swung and missed, the razors flashing in the sun. Tucker repeated the feint twice, circling each time, forcing the man to attack slightly off balance. The third time, the man caught a piece of Tucker's upper arm, the multiple razors slicing through the shirt and into his skin. The biker jerked his weapon back in a spray of blood and flesh. Tucker's arm hurt but the pain was a separate thing, like bad weather.

He could see the second biker coming around the toolhouse, followed by other men. Tucker feinted again and the big man slashed but Tucker parried with his forearm, the thick magazines catching the razors, trapping the weapon long enough to step inside the biker's reach and cut him deep and hard across the belly with the sharpened footrest. The big man yanked his weapon free of the magazine pages. He tried to slash but gray intestines were spilling out of his shirt amid yellow fat and blood. His knees collapsed and he sat, clasping both arms across his stomach.

Tucker sensed the second biker behind him and twisted his body but felt a sudden pain in his lower back. The layer of magazines had diverted the blade from his kidney, but it slid into his body below his ribs. He jerked his right elbow backward, forcing the biker to retreat. Tucker spun and lunged, but the man sidestepped and slashed Tucker's torso, a downward motion that cut his chest, split his shirt, and sliced through the magazines. A sheaf of pages blew into the air as if Tucker were bleeding paper. He hopped back, his left arm hanging loosely, his hand red with blood dripping to the ground. The wound on his chest was not too deep.

The biker crouched low, holding the blade underhand in front of him. He made a quick lunge at Tucker's face, then slashed down, cutting away a section of magazine, leaving a thin red stripe along his belly. Tucker charged the man, pinning his knife arm between their bodies, ramming the man into the toolshed wall. He stabbed the man twice in the side but the makeshift blade was too short to reach the lungs. He rammed his knee between the biker's legs, stepped back, and chopped at the man's face, seeing part of his nose fly away in a gout of blood. Tucker felt a sudden blow to his head and turned to see a guard clubbing him. He fell, drawing his body into a protective ball, covered his head, and was beaten unconscious. He awoke in the prison infirmary.

In his weakened state Tucker understood that he was vulnerable to further attack. At night he moved to a different bed and watched his former spot, the hard mattress and gray sheets, but nobody arrived to kill him. He was always on the verge of sleep, a middle area that provided no rest. He could nap for minutes at a time, then jerk awake. Needing more time to recuperate, he feigned remorse to the medical personnel and they sent for the chaplain, a priest. Tucker wasn't sure what a Catholic was and lumped him in with his generalized knowledge of religion in the hills—the Lord's touch, talking in tongues, the gyrations of people in the aisle. The priest was an old man with liquor on his breath. At times he seemed in despair and Tucker felt sorry for him. He decided to talk.

"There was Adam and Eve," Tucker said. "Then two boys."

"Yes."

"Cain killed Abel. Then Cain got married and had kids."

The priest nodded. Inmates often suggested they were sons of Cain to justify crimes, especially homicide.

"Then," Tucker said, "where'd Cain's wife come from?"

The priest never visited him again. In his absence, Tucker retreated further into himself while increasing his vigilance. He felt like a sniper on a hillside looking through the scope of a rifle—simultaneously close and far. He thought often of his wife and family. He missed Big Billy most, someone he could talk to with trust, the son who never aged. Without Big Billy's perpetual listening ear, there was no one for him.

After his recovery he was shuttled to the maximum-security facility at Eddyville with five years added to his sentence. The Dayton Satans sent two men for him in the showers. Tucker dispatched one with a sock filled with bars of soap, and rammed the other man's head into a sink until an eye popped from its socket. Tucker turned on all the hot water and used the steam as cover to get back to his cell. The bikers left him alone after that. Everyone did. He served the rest of his time without incident, working in the laundry. At night he made plans for the ten thousand dollars waiting for him upon release.

1971

Chapter Ten

Tucker stepped outside the walls of the Kentucky State Penitentiary and blinked at the vast horizon. A long broken cloud angled across the sky, its bottom edged with gray. He inhaled deeply, savoring the pungent scent of a river. Even in the exercise yard, the air was stale as if an invisible lid lay over the space. The cells were worse. At times he'd wondered if he got enough oxygen, if it was possible for hundreds of men breathing the same air to leach away its value. The gate slammed shut behind him.

He had thirty-four dollars and clothes that didn't fit, having gained weight from a steady diet of starch. He descended the grassless slope to the longest car he'd ever seen, red with a thin white stripe running the length of the body. The bumper reflected the sky.

A man in his early twenties leaned against the car, smoking a cigarette cupped in his hand. He was tall but torso-shy, all the height in his legs. He wore a narrow-brimmed high-crowned hat, a white T-shirt under a partly buttoned yellow shirt, and over that a blue jean jacket.

"You Tucker?" the man said.

Tucker nodded.

"I'm Jimmy. Where's your duffel at?"

Tucker shook his head. Jimmy tilted slightly sidewise to spit between his teeth in a way Tucker recognized as requiring hours of practice. He'd never understood people who threw so much time into something with no purpose.

"Reckon you need some clothes," Jimmy said. "I know just the place to go. Bought me this fee-dora in town today."

He removed his hat and admired it, turning it in the sun, flicking away imaginary dust. He stroked its crease gently. Tucker didn't move. If Beanpole had sent this guy, he'd offer proof. Jimmy adjusted the hat to his skull at an angle he seemed to consider stylish.

"You like it?" Jimmy said.

"You need another one."

"An extra in case it gets dirty?"

"One to shit in," Tucker said. "And another one to cover it up with."

Jimmy dropped his cigarette. He set his boots firmly, one slightly in front of the other, and rolled his broad shoulders. That's all it usually took to intimidate men, especially little bastards gone to fat. Beanpole had warned him not to underestimate Tucker, but the hat was a damn twenty-five-dollar imported Borsalino. He gave Tucker his hardest glare. Tucker didn't flinch or look away. Figuring to give him another chance, Jimmy removed the hat from his head and tipped it to the light.

"Man at the store said it sparkled with a gem-like radiance," he said, "I can see it. Can you? A gem-like radiance."

Tucker reached for the hat and sure enough the overgrown boy gave it to him. Tucker placed it over his right hand, made a fist inside the hat and hit Jimmy just below his breastbone. Jimmy folded in half. His backside bounced off the car and he dropped to his knees. He regained his breath enough to vomit a thin stream of diner eggs into the dirt, careful not to splash the hat.

"Got anything for me?" Tucker said.

"Glove box," Jimmy gasped.

Tucker stepped around the car and opened the compartment. It contained a carton of Lucky cigarettes, and an envelope with fifty dollars and a printed note: MORE LATER. GO EASY ON JIMMY. WIFE'S BROTHER'S BOY. It was unsigned, testament to Beanpole's wariness of the law. A carton was worth a lot of money inside and Tucker brushed the thought away—from now on he could smoke as many as he wanted and use actual cash for currency.

Tucker wondered if Beanpole's sending this dolt was a sign of disrespect. More likely it was an opportunity to get rid of Jimmy for a day or two. If Beanpole wanted to convey a message, nobody would've been waiting outside the prison. Either he didn't trust his nephew with money, or Beanpole wanted to pay him in person.

Tucker helped the boy to his feet.

"Didn't have to do my hat that way," Jimmy said.

"Should've told me you was Beanpole's nephew."

"I'm sick of folks only knowing that. Beanpole's bucket boy. Thought maybe I'd just be Jimmy with somebody new."

Tucker realized the boy resented his uncle and filed the information away. Jimmy tenderly pressed his stomach, then brushed the Borsalino of dust that was no longer imaginary. He fitted it to his head at a cocky slant.

"Where to first?" Jimmy said. "Whorehouse or haberdasher?"

"A what?" Tucker wondered if he was going to have to hit him again.

"Haberdasher. They got men's clothes."

"Gun," Tucker said. "And a knife."

They drove to the nearest town of Eddyville. At a men's store he bought work clothes, a thick belt, and heavy brogans. Most of the jackets were Eisenhower style with a short waist that allowed wind to cut across his particulars. He bought a wool-lined denim coat long enough to cover a gun. The salesman offered a deal on a pair of gloves that Tucker refused, having never worn a pair in his life. If a man couldn't work his fingers in cold weather, he wasn't worth a nickel.

They entered Howorth's Hardware Store, where a woman in her forties stood behind a multi-drawer cash register made of oak and marble. Beside her was a wooden barrel of pickles. Her hair swirled into a hybrid between a bun and a hive, each strand drawn tight from her scalp. She wore a smock over a floral blouse that covered what appeared to be the armature of a large brassiere. Jimmy addressed her chest and asked for guns.

"See Mr. Howorth in the back," she said, and tapped a small silver bell twice. The sharp peal drifted in the air. When the sound dissipated, she chimed the bell three more times.

"Are you Mrs. Howorth?" Jimmy said with a leer he'd practiced in a bathroom mirror.

The woman moved her tight lips in the semblance of a smile and nodded. Jimmy kicked the barrel lightly, careful not to scuff his boot.

"You like pickles?" he said. "A good-size pickle?"

Tucker turned away and walked a dimly lit aisle between metal bins containing hundreds of pipe fittings. Jimmy followed. His boot heels had metal taps that rang with each step, announcing his progress like a belled cat.

"Them older ladies got the biggest dugs ever was," Jimmy said.

"Don't talk," Tucker said.

Jimmy gritted his teeth to quell a response. All his life he'd heard variations of shut up, hush up, quiet down, and his mother's firm "Enough," but no one had ever ordered him not to talk. He didn't like it. He had a right to talk, same as any man, but he'd hold off for a few minutes at least.

The rear of the store held a long slab of white oak, marred by stains and nicks. Rifles and pistols lined the back wall, hanging on wooden pegs wrapped with cotton to prevent them from scratching the gunmetal. In the middle of the wall was an open doorway where a man in a greasy apron stood. He was tall with long hands, slim-fingered as a banjo picker. Pushed up on his balding head was a special set of glasses that magnified small work. His grandfather had started the store and his father had nearly run it into the ground by making bad deals while drunk. It had fallen to him to stave off the creditors. He'd made a few mistakes, including a marriage to a woman he didn't like. The store's legacy would end with him and when the time came he wanted to go out big. He planned on disappearing to Myrtle Beach alone.

"Fellers," he said. "What can I do you for?"

"Needing me a pistol," Tucker said.

"Call me Freddy Three on account of I'm the third Frederick Howorth. Everybody does, or just call me Three. I'll answer to damn near anything. But I got to ask you something you might not like. Half the town works at the pen. And I know all of them. My opinion, you got the look of someone who might've just got out."

Tucker waited for the man to say whatever was on his mind. Beside him he felt Jimmy's tension spread like clay mud in rain, the kind that can catch a man's foot and pull his boot off with the next step.

"I don't like being the one to tell you this," Howorth said, "but there's many a man who got turned loose and bought a gun in town and held the place up. Way it is, nobody in town will sell a gun to a man fresh out. It's not me. It's the town. I can't help it."

"How about I buy one," Jimmy said. "I ain't been inside."

"That's a way around it, sure enough. But it's a little too late. I'm sorry. I surely am. I'm a businessman and don't like turning away business. But that's the way it is."

At waist level beneath the man's apron Tucker saw the bulge of a pistol. He figured a cut-down shotgun lay just out of sight under the counter. He turned away, aware of the man's vision boring into his back as he walked the length of the store. Tucker gave Mrs. Howorth a polite nod and pushed the door open. He heard Jimmy stop. Tucker turned and watched him unzip his pants and reach inside his fly, take a half-step to the pickle barrel and tip forward on his toes. Quick as a gnat, Mrs. Howorth withdrew a small-caliber revolver and aimed it at his chest. Jimmy halted, back arched and heels lifted, his body seeming to freeze in place. He scooted backward and out the open door.

On the sidewalk Jimmy zipped his pants and devoted nearly a minute to adjusting his belt buckle. It was shaped like a silver horseshoe glinting in the sun. Tucker hoped it still had some luck because the boy needed all he could get.

"You mad at me?" Jimmy said.

"No," Tucker said. "I don't like pickles."

"Damn, she pulled that gun slicker than owl grease. Some kind of little stinger, wasn't it."

"Looked like a thirty-two," Tucker said.

"See how fast I got my peter out? It's not wearing under-drawers that does it."

"You saying you ain't got no drawers on?"

"Waste of money," Jimmy said. "If you wipe, who needs them?"

He laughed, his face losing all the forced toughness and transforming to a child wanting approval for a failed prank.

"God-double-damn," Jimmy said, "that's the kind of woman I been wanting. Stacked up like a brick shit house and gun-handy as a deputy."

"Uh-huh," Tucker said. "You best go back to not talking for a spell."

"Okay. Where to now?"

"Next town toward home. I ain't spending another penny here."

They drove highway 62 to the town of Princeton and bought a gun without incident, a long-barreled Colt thirty-eight Police Special. A four-inch barrel would hide better, but Tucker liked the idea of wearing the same gun as lawmen. They stopped at a roadside diner called the Trixie Grill and took a booth, sitting in their jackets and hats, countrymen in town. Tucker ordered fried chicken, green beans, cornbread and coffee. Jimmy refilled his empty stomach with another breakfast.

Clad in a white dress, lightly stained from food, the waitress walked briskly away, nylons brushing her thighs with every step. Her dark hair was pulled back in a ponytail, the sides held by bobby pins tipped with plastic. Tucker couldn't recall the last time he'd seen bobby pins, didn't know he'd missed them. He watched her hips twitch. From the dormant region below his belt he felt a vague heat.

The waitress brought their meals on heavy ceramic plates and refilled their coffee. Tucker began eating in a methodical way, forearms on the table to guard his food, one hand holding the edge of the plate in case he needed a weapon. He didn't think he'd ever eaten better chicken. Six years he'd waited for cornbread and it was too dry.

Between Princeton and Elizabethtown they stopped twice for Tucker to avail himself of gas station facilities, the food having slid through his bowels like Sherman through Georgia. After years of rocky constipation from prison chow, his guts had turned sloppy. Jimmy knew better than to comment. Growing big early and able to whip his buddies in a fistfight wasn't enough to match Tucker, whose age was indeterminate and size misleading. His damn eyes didn't even pair up. Worse, the son of a bitch had armed himself.

Jimmy traveled with a pistol under the seat but it had slid along the floorboards out of reach, occasionally clanking against an empty Coca-Cola bottle with a dull sound that irritated him. He'd imagined a gallivanting journey with a real outlaw, first to a bootlegger, then to a whorehouse. But all Tucker wanted to do was chain-smoke and stare out the window. Not even ten years older than Jimmy, he'd already been to war and prison. Tucker ran shine at the tail end of the wild times, earned Uncle Beanpole's respect, and had a reputation for toughness and honor. Frustrated by his inability to impress the man, Jimmy felt restless. Nothing had worked except his thwarted impulse to piss in the pickles, which seemed to amuse Tucker into a short-term softening that had already passed.

He straddled a flattened squirrel, then swerved to run over a snake warming itself on the blacktop's edge. In the rear-view mirror he grinned as it writhed, its back end flopping.

"Got him," he said. "I pure despise a snake. You see his tail flopping?"

"It's a snake. Pretty much all tail."

"How's your guts holding up?" Jimmy said.

"Better."

"Good," Jimmy said. "What was it like? In Eddyville I mean."

Tucker slowly counted to a hundred before answering.

"First day," Tucker said, "they put me in a cell with the biggest man I ever saw. Name of Bullethead. His head went up to a point, more like a howitzer shell than a bullet, but I didn't say nothing on that."

"Showed good sense there," Jimmy said.

"One ear gone, just a hole in the side of that head."

"Did he have a fake one?"

Tucker lapsed into silence, wondering how the boy had got this far in life. Tucker reached into his shirt pocket and removed a cigarette from the pack. It was a prison method of getting a smoke that prevented people from seeing a pack and bumming one. He turned his head to light it, the Zippo flaring, his hand cupped to hide his grin.

"Well," Jimmy said. "What happened?"

"He said with two to a cell, one was a husband and the other a wife. Said the new guy got to pick being a husband or a wife."

Tucker stopped talking and waited, knowing he wouldn't have to wait very long for Jimmy to ask the obvious. It took less than ten seconds.

"What'd you pick?" Jimmy said.

"I told him I'd just as soon be the husband."

"No shit," Jimmy said. "What'd he do?"

"Well, he looked at me a minute. And he said, all right then, come over here and meet your wife's pecker."

"What'd you do?"

Tucker blew smoke and squinted as the wind flung it back in his eyes. The cigarette was burning faster on the side facing the window and he dabbed spit on it to even the fire.

"Thing is, Jimmy, what would you do?"

Jimmy adjusted his posture and gripped the steering wheel tightly. The answer was clear, and he tried to work through Tucker's words to figure out if it was a trick question. His brother used to do that when they were kids, and still did upon occasion—ask questions with no good answer. It occurred to him that Tucker was making a comment about his masculinity. The idea made Jimmy mad.

"I like women," he yelled. "All of them—tall, short, old, young, fat, and skinny. By God, I'd push my girlfriend out a window to fuck someone else."

"You got a girlfriend?"

"No. But I ain't no damn cake boy."

"Nobody said you was."

Tucker gave a slight grin. Provoking this boy was easy. His brain was a dam missing a river. Tucker laughed.

"It ain't all that funny," Jimmy said.

"Maybe not. But you getting mad was."

"My brother used to do me that way. I never liked it."

"Big brother, I bet."

"That's right," Jimmy said. "Two years older. James was always telling me some bullshit."

"Say your brother's name is James?"

Jimmy nodded.

"You do know," Tucker said, "that's the same as Jimmy."

"I heard that. But I don't reckon my folks did. They liked both names. You got a thing to say about that?"

Tucker shook his head. He lit another Lucky and watched the land slide by. Jimmy hadn't been raised right and Tucker worried about his own son growing up without a father. Rhonda had sent him a grainy black-and-white photograph of a fine-looking child, hair white as an old man's. Tucker never showed the photo to anyone but looked at it every night.

Prison had sped the passage of time even as it moved at a slow pace. He decided not to run shine anymore. With the ten thousand dollars Beanpole owed him, he'd be able to get by for years. He could garden and hunt small game for the table, raise tobacco for cash, get a few chickens and hogs and one good cow. He mainly looked forward to seeing Rhonda and the kids.

Chapter Eleven

Zeph Tolliver rose at sunrise every day, observing an amalgam of his own inner clock and the territorial calling of songbirds in the woods surrounding his house. He lay in bed, listening for the creak of his mother's rocking chair on the porch. Beulah wore work pants, the only woman on the hill who did. She rolled the cuff of one pants leg to form a cotton trough for flicking the ash from her cigarettes, painstakingly hand-rolled with gumless OCB papers.

Zeph rose and dressed and joined his mother. She faced him with her opaque eyes, blind from cataracts. A patch of ground fog lay in a low dip of land, the rest of the mist already swirling away. Golden light filtered through the autumn trees.

"Turned off cold," she said. "What's the leaves doing?"

"Softwoods are yellowing on."

"Poplar?"

"Mostly all dropped. A few sugar maples."

"Ones facing west?"

"That's right. Without no hill blocking the sun."

"One good rain will knock half down."

"Reckon," he said. "You calling for it?"

"Not yet, I ain't. But three, four days."

They drank coffee. Her skills at weather had increased with age. For more than seventy years people had asked Zeph what his mother was calling for, and she was seldom wrong. Zeph heard the intermittent drilling of flickers seeking bugs.

"Hard as they hit a tree," his mother said. "I don't know why their eyes don't pop right out of their heads."

"Yep," Zeph said.

She'd gotten fixated on sight since losing hers and lately he'd begun worrying she was going around the bend. Even blind she walked the field beyond the house, sometimes entering the woods at night.

"How high's that grass getting to be past the old smokehouse?" she said.

She pointed the correct direction and he looked at the grass moving in the breeze, the swaying tops heavily furred by seed.

"Past knee-high," he said.

"Is it fell over yet?"

"Not yet," he said. "I got to go, Mom."

She nodded, a nearly imperceptible motion. Creases lined her face like old bark. Her silver hair fell down her back to her waist. He wondered how much his mother could see, if it came and went, if she still recognized his features. Lately she'd begun touching his face as if memory seeped through her fingertips.

He drove his old truck to a dirt road, then followed the ridge downslope to the blacktop. A narrow lane ran behind the elementary school. Beyond it ran the shallow creek, now reduced to a few separate pools in which minnows and crawdads struggled to survive. Increments of water evaporated each day, evidenced by a fresh rim of dirt around the edges. Zeph understood that water slowly vanished, drawn into the sky and returning as rain. He wondered what kind of schedule evaporation ran on, how wind could blow invisible water to another part of the county.

In fifteen minutes he'd hear the principal's car. For all his sixty-two years, Zeph had never owned a watch but always knew the time, an essentially useless skill. He sat and worried about his mother. Beulah had been the most sought after granny-woman in the hills until a problem birth made her decide to quit. Zeph was the youngest and she taught him about the woods, lessons she'd learned from her grandmother: Eat poke root but not the berries, plant crop so it flowers in the new moon, let dipper gourds get frosted on twice to harden their shell. Now she was slipping away, her body and mind dwindling daily, her knowledge of the hills evaporating like the creek.

Children who lived on the hill walked to school, including Jo, who accompanied her six-year-old brother along a path through the woods. She'd felt funny for a few days and this morning she'd barely been able to move, cramped bad in the belly. In science class she stood abruptly and left for the restroom, hurrying along the school's dim hall. She hadn't eaten breakfast, but felt as if she'd messed herself. She pushed open the restroom door, grateful that no one else was there, and lifted her dress. Her underpants were soaked with blood. Jo cleaned herself with an entire roll of toilet paper, then prayed. She begged God to let her live through the day. She wanted to be alive when her father got home from prison.

During lunch break, her teacher found her.

"Oh my dear Lord," Mrs. Crawford said. "You poor thing."

"Am I going to die?"

"No, honey. You got your monthlies is all."

Mrs. Crawford hugged Jo awkwardly and studied her tear-stained face, the tension of misery etched into her skin.

"Didn't anyone tell you about this?" Mrs. Crawford said.

Jo shook her head.

"Let's get you cleaned up."

Jo nodded. She trusted the teacher but decided to continue praying in case she was wrong. Mrs. Crawford used hand towels to daub the blood, explaining in halting terms that what Jo had undergone was perfectly normal, that it happened to all girls and would continue until she was much older. Jo listened quietly. It seemed preposterous and unfair but at least she wasn't dying.

"We need to get you home," Mrs. Crawford said. "We'll call your mother."

"Ain't got a phone," Jo said.

"All right, we'll call a neighbor then."

"They ain't none right close."

They walked to the principal's office, where Mrs. Crawford explained the situation to Mr. Lawton. He sent her to the second-grade classroom for Jo's little brother. Mr. Lawton went to the boiler room and asked Zeph to drive the kids home.

Zeph led the children outside, unable to recall the last time he had a passenger. Mainly he used the truck as storage for scrap metal, lumber, and tools. The tailgate wouldn't latch correctly and he'd tied it off with bailing wire. Zeph opened the passenger door by lifting hard on the handle, and giving it a yank that released flakes of chrome. A tattered sheet lay in creased wrinkles over the upholstering. The boy climbed in and scooted over for his sister. Zeph closed the door, its hinges shrill in the still air. He circled the truck and slid behind the wheel.

Zeph realized how much the boy resembled his father when he was a sprout—the nearly perfectly rounded skull with ears protruding like dippers cocked forward, the sharp eyes and sly mouth. His hair was cut short, the scalp appearing to glow from the blond hair.

"You'uns are Tuckers, ain't you," Zeph said.

The boy nodded.

"You his first boy?" Zeph said.

The boy shook his head and Zeph realized his error. He drove onto the blacktop. "You're his first boy, his second boy, and the last one all rolled together, ain't you. What's your name?"

"Shiny."

"Like a new penny shiny?" Zeph said.

"On account of my head."

"Well, I'm danged. You're right. It does shine. About like a full moon."

"Mommy says Daddy named me it."

"All right, Shiny. Can you drive a truck?"

"No. I'm too little."

"Maybe you are. But if you was to tie some sticks to your legs, why you'd be able to reach the pedals."

The boy looked at the floorboards as if measuring the distance. Zeph grinned and placed his palm on the gearshift, a long rod with a knob he'd carved from a hickory knot.

"This here's how you change gears to go faster. You grab this metal pole here. It'll shake but won't hurt."

The boy tentatively grasped the gearshift, feeling the vibration travel along his arm, through his shoulder, and into his chest. It was like holding something alive and strong. Standing on the seat, he placed his weight on his toes and leaned forward until he could peer through the windshield. The black metal hood glinted in the sun. Shiny turned to his sister in triumph, but she was sick. Their mother got the vapors and took to the bed for weeks, and he hoped it wasn't the same and it wasn't catchy. He didn't know what the vapors were but the result left him on his own for days.

He could eat what he wanted, climb all the trees he felt like, and wander the woods till dark.

"Hold on tight," Zeph said, "I got to pull your hill."

Shiny nodded, eyes wide. Zeph downshifted, wishing the truck had one more lower drive. The hill slanted steep and scrabbly as if God was mad the day he laid the land out. The road rose sharply, forcing Zeph to find the precise point of acceleration where the truck would continue without spinning out. Junk in the truck bed slid backward and struck the tailgate. The wire snapped, the gate dropped, and cargo spilled into the road. Zeph hunched over the wheel. If he stopped, he'd lose all momentum. The road made a hard turn and vanished, grown over at the only semi-level spot, but Zeph continued through a stand of softwoods. Branches scraped the cab, leaving torn leaves on the windshield. Zeph swerved around a young hornbeam tree that had gained sufficient hold in what passed for the road.

The pickup broke through the final overhang of maple into the sudden light of midday. Weeds and brush grew in a yard that ended at the house. Zeph honked the horn twice in standard greeting. He drove through the yard and parked near the porch with the passenger door facing the house to make it easier on the girl.

Inside, Rhonda heard the engine followed by the horn. She was looking at the dull mirror in the bathroom. One edge rippled like water. Flecks of silver had fallen away, revealing the flat black surface behind. She tucked hair behind an ear and smoothed her dress.

Six years ago, Beanpole's wife had visited to explain that Tucker would be kept in prison longer—it wasn't Tucker's fault, just bad luck. Rhonda waited season by season, telling her son stories about his father so he wouldn't forget he had one. She maintained the family as best she could but neglected the house and property, planting a smaller garden every year. She'd gained weight and lost weight, and been unbearably sad.

Last week Beanpole's wife came by and said he'd sent a man to Eddyville to fetch Tucker. Rhonda cleaned the house and listened to the radio. She imagined her husband striding across the yard to see them waiting on the porch, Rhonda standing in the middle, her hands resting on her children's shoulders. They'd all look at each other, smiling and happy at last.

This fantasy was crucial to her, especially the joy that Tucker would feel. She'd planned several ways to tell him that Bessie, Ida, Velmey, and Big Billy were gone. She blamed herself and feared he would, too. She'd let her children be hauled away by officials of the state—a man in a suit, three men in white hospital clothes, and a persnickety woman who never looked Rhonda in the eye. Rhonda asked about Hattie, her previous social worker, and the woman in the dress said she'd quit.

Three men carried the girls to a modified van and belted them into special seats. A separate vehicle, an ambulance with the emergency lights removed, was designated for Big Billy. After a great deal of hemming and hawing, the men moved Big Billy onto a gurney they'd wheeled into the house. One man was in charge of his head. Big Billy didn't make a sound or move, his limbs devoid of muscle, his eyes unseeing. Rhonda stared at his feet, his soft precious feet, and leaped from the chair. She grabbed the end of the gurney and clenched it tightly. The men tugged, but she wouldn't release it. The man in the suit gave an order and one man held Rhonda's arms while the others pried her fingers free, one by one. She collapsed on the floor. Through the open door she watched the men load Big Billy into the back of the vehicle like freight. The woman asked for signatures on twelve forms, three for each child, then left. For the next seven months Rhonda didn't leave her bed and rarely ate. Daily she aimed fierce recriminations at herself—she shouldn't have let it happen, she shouldn't have signed those papers, she shouldn't have answered the door.

Rhonda heard a car door open outside and knew her husband was finally home. She checked her lipstick one more time, lifting her lips to make sure none was on her teeth. Her body felt light and airy as a milkweed pod. Rhonda yearned for the coarse feel of his face on her neck, his callused fingers brushing her shoulders, arms, and thighs. It'd been a long six years of celibacy. She hoped everything still worked right, that the front of her behind hadn't dried up.

She walked briskly through the house, moving with purpose for the first time in years. Everything was tidy and in its place. She stepped onto the porch, immediately perplexed, then alarmed. Instead of her husband, old Zeph stood in the yard. His arm was propped like a handle for Jo to hold as she slid from the bench seat, her feet reaching for the side step. Behind her, Shiny stood in the truck, grinning like a possum.

Rhonda had experienced disappointment enough times that its quick arrival was familiar, something she knew how to endure.

"Shiny, get out of that truck and help your sister," she said. "Zeph, what is it—chicken pox, mumps, or measles?"

Zeph shrugged and shook his head. Jo stood unsteadily on the dirt, clinging to his arm. Blood trickled down her leg and Rhonda understood that she had waited too long to talk to Jo, that her daughter had somehow gotten old enough to menstruate. Zeph patted Jo's hand until she released him, leaving crescent imprints of her nails in his skin. Rhonda led Jo into the house with Shiny following.

Zeph looked around, unsure what to do. He wanted to leave but Rhonda might need to send him for a doctor. He wondered how long he should wait.

Chapter Twelve

Jimmy was tired of Tucker's long silences and occasional orders—turn off the radio, go this way, drive slow. A car like his needed to move and Jimmy wanted to prove his skill to the man considered the best driver in the hills. They stopped for gas and Jimmy's metal heel taps rattled on the concrete as he walked inside the station to pay.

Tucker closed his eyes and listened for his return, trying to predict when Jimmy would open the car door. He guessed right within two seconds.

"What do you wear them heel taps for?" Tucker said.

"So folks know it's me," Jimmy said. "They hear them taps, they by God know they're in for trouble."

"Gives a man plenty of time to hide. Or run away."

"Everybody runs from me," Jimmy said.

"You ever been in a knife fight?"

"Once or twice," Jimmy lied. "Ain't everybody?"

"The way you win a knife fight is not show the knife. It's the same with heel taps. You can't surprise nobody."

"I ain't fighting with my boots."

"You got me there, Jimmy."

Jimmy drove, more irritated than ever. The way Tucker acted, he thought he was shit on a stick, and would be if he had a peg leg. Jimmy wanted to eat at the window diner in Salt Lick, the best food around, and the site of a murder where the man got away. Tucker flatly refused. The detour added two hours around Salt Lick, then the son-of-a-bitch wanted to drive slow as an old lady through Morehead, along Railroad Street, then back on Main Street, and Railroad Street again. Town had one movie theater, a pool hall, a bowling alley, and a couple of restaurants, all of which Tucker ignored. He seemed to be looking for something and when Jimmy asked what it was, Tucker said, "Change."

"You'd best look in seat cushions," Jimmy said. "You'll find more change there than town."

Jimmy laughed at what he considered a pretty good joke. Tucker never smiled or said a word. Jimmy left the blacktop and crossed the creek on an oak bridge. It had been built of green lumber, bowed and warped, the boards themselves drawn far apart from each other. Jimmy winced each time the tires bounced across the wide cracks. Two hollers up, he turned onto the remnants of a dirt lane. Poke encroached the edges, fighting milkweed for water and light. The center of the road was humped by horseweed, raising the earth in spots that scraped the undercarriage. He stopped at the foot of the steep slope to Beanpole's old house, where Tucker's family lived. No one had maintained the road since Beanpole moved out.

"Uh-uh," Jimmy said. "Ain't about to try and pull that. It's half creek, half road, and half gully."

"That's too many halfs," Tucker said.

He left the car and Jimmy watched him go, disgusted that Tucker hadn't looked at him or thanked him for the ride. Worst of all, Jimmy had to scoot awkwardly across the bench seat to close the passenger door. Tucker hardly talked and then made no sense. The way Jimmy saw it, a man couldn't get enough halfs. The more you had, the more chance to make a whole. He turned the volume high on the radio and hoped it was loud enough to scare a snake into biting Tucker. He backed down the road, searching for a wide place to turn around.

Tucker climbed the hill, feeling the tightness in his legs, familiar and comfortable after five years of walking on flat concrete. He knew the radio sound was aimed at him and chuckled silently. One day someone would beat that boy into a cripple, but not Tucker. The satisfaction wasn't worth prison and he was never going back.

Midway up the hill was a slight turn, then an increase in the steepness. Tucker halted, surprised at the amount of junk scattered in the road: a rotted tire on an old rim, roofing tin rusted through in spots, several lengths of lumber, a concrete block, and a carburetor. An engine sounded from above, an old V-8 straining in first gear, the brake pads shrieking against bare metal. Tucker sidestepped swiftly into the woods.

A late-1930s Ford pickup appeared from up the hill, wheels skidding as the driver braked to avoid the junk in the road. The truck halted at an angle, the front end aimed away from the edge of the hill. No man could have surprised Tucker more than Zeph. He was too old to be chasing after Rhonda and too gentle for trouble. Tucker had known him all his life. His mother had grannied Tucker into the world, and Big Billy, too.

Tucker moved into view.

"Hey, Zeph," he called.

Zeph nodded once in greeting.

"This stuff in the road yours?" Tucker said.

"Fell out on the way up," Zeph said. "I can't get past it."

"You want any of it?"

"Lumber, maybe."

Tucker nodded and began throwing the debris over the hill. He carried four oak boards, fifty years old by the width and weight of them, and placed them in the truck bed. He lifted the tailgate and tied the baling wire.

"Ort to do her till you get home," he said.

"Appreciate it," Zeph said. "I'd give you a ride but I'm heading the wrong direction."

"It's good to see you're still on your hind legs."

"Ain't just me. Mommy's alive, too."

"Getting up there, ain't she," Tucker said. "How old is she, a hundred?"

"Ninety-seven or ninety-nine. She was born a odd-numbered year and ain't for sure which one it was."

"Come Judgment Day, the angels will knock her in the head to get her to go, my opinion."

Zeph nodded.

"What are you doing up at the house?" Tucker said.

"Brung them kids home from school. Your girl's sick. That boy is nigh ready to start driving."

"Driving."

"He ain't a-feared of it."

"Well," Tucker said. "I'd best get up there. Tell your mom hidy for me."

"You might want to get behind me. Ain't for sure which way this rig'll go when I let the brake off."

Zeph waited until Tucker was clear, then started cutting the wheel and easing pressure on the brake. The truck jolted, tried to stall, backfired, then continued downhill. The Tuckers were a good bunch with bad luck, same as a lot of hill families. You helped when you could, but he hoped he was clear of the Tuckers for good. Trouble came their way like sideways wind in winter.

At the top of what passed for a driveway Tucker stood in the woods and watched the house. Five and a half years was long enough for the dogs to forget him and he didn't want to fight his own animals. He moved closer, waiting for them, thinking maybe they knew his smell, then realized there were no dogs. He stepped into the yard, clumped by weeds, a car with two flat tires beneath a tree. Ivy tangled the shed. He remembered sitting on the same porch making a deal with Beanpole.

In prison Tucker had resisted the impulse to think about his return. It was a dangerous habit that let vigilance erode.

He'd witnessed the results in other men, a precursor to despair. Nevertheless, he succumbed every few months, indulging the fantasy of his triumphant return: his wife graceful and radiant, the children miraculously cured of ailment, Jo at the top of her class, Shiny confident and tall.

Now he looked at the house and knew something was wrong. The porch step was split, the wood trim paint-peeled. Leaves overflowed the gutters. The downspout was missing. A ripple of anxiety passed through his body. He opened the door and yelled a greeting.

The house held a surprising stillness that was contrary to the perpetual clangor of prison, the howling men. He checked Big Billy's spot but the crib bed was gone. Rhonda slowly descended the stairs, hand against the wall. There was no rail and she took each step carefully as if it were her first time on steps. Tucker thought she was beautiful, unchanged, dark hair wisping from a clip. She wore a dress. Upon reaching the floor she moved fast, her arms around him in a hug tighter than he'd ever felt. A deep tension loosened in his body as if each muscle were a leaf shock on a run-car, easing pressure with removal of the load. He squeezed her until she gasped. He had the sensation that the two of them were a single tree split by weather, the exposed bark finding itself and fusing. The past few years seemed to evaporate from his body.

He opened his eyes without realizing he'd closed them and saw a boy standing on the steps, eyes wide.

"Shiny," he said, "is that you?"

The boy ran to him, wrapping his small arms around his father's leg. Tucker placed his hand on his son's shoulder. The three of them stood, swaying slightly. Tucker relaxed his grip.

"Where's Big Billy," he said. "Where's Jo?"

"She's sick," Rhonda said.

"Bad sick?"

"No, she's in her flowers."

"How can that be? She ain't but what, eleven?"

"Just shy of thirteen," Rhonda said. "It's about right."

Tucker frowned. He'd left a girl who'd become a woman. The baby boy was three feet tall with a grin full of teeth. Tucker felt momentarily dizzy.

"Big Billy," he said. "Where is he?"

"Shiny," Rhonda said. "Go check on Jo. Take her some water and stay in your room."

Tucker nodded once to his son, who reluctantly left. Rhonda walked to the couch and sat.

"A lot's happened," she said. "Most not good."

"Where's Big Billy?"

"The state took him. The babies, too. I didn't have no choice."

"Who?" he said. "Who did it?"

"I don't know. One was a doctor. I never seen the rest of them before."

"It wasn't that woman used to come?"

"No, she quit. Then after four years, a couple of new ones showed up. The next spring they come and took Big

Billy and the girls. I set here and let them, Tucker. I let them carry my babies off. I'm sorry. I'm so sorry."

He felt bewildered, as if he inhabited someone else's life. The battered furnishings were familiar but not the contour of the walls, the layout of the house. In prison he'd led a kind of semi-life and now he was a stranger in his own home. He left the house. His favorite spot was five miles away by car, three if he walked. He entered the woods and climbed the slope where it met the ridge. Tucker walked in a fury, not seeing the leaves or hearing the birds, his woods skills rusty from years of concrete. He couldn't focus his mind. He felt betrayed and trapped. He'd abandoned his family and this was the penalty—losing four kids. His stomach churned as if controlled by a mechanical crank. Sweat coated him. He began removing his clothes—jacket, shirt, and undershirt—and flung them into the woods. At the top of the ridgeline above his old house, he began a slow descent and went unerringly to his spot.

Leaves covered the rock. He kicked aside the brush, panting from exertion, having smoked too much with little exercise for five years. He sat on the rock. His spot. Nothing had changed here. He removed his boots and socks, then his pants. His body continued to feel aflame. Carefully placing the pistol in a boot, he collected the decayed leaves and earth in his hands and rubbed the cool loam on his skin. A thorn ripped a gash that he didn't feel. His body was far away from his mind. He leaned back and stared at a patch of sky through the intertwining limbs. Nothing made sense. He sat for an hour without moving, then stood abruptly, put on his boots, and carried his pistol down the hill to the edge of the woods.

The old house he'd spent months repairing fourteen years before stood as he remembered it, now with a new roof. The old porch had been torn away and replaced by one with brick posts and steps. The yard was bigger, the grass cropped and uniform. The woods behind the house were clear-cut. White gravel covered the driveway, ending in an oblong area bordered with old railroad ties. The pines he'd planted as a winter windbreak had quadrupled in height.

When they'd traded houses, Beanpole and his wife had moved nearer to their grandkids. Tucker didn't know who lived here now. He experienced a sudden impulse to walk down there and shoot everyone inside, then lie down and sleep. But he had no means of getting away, and worse, he was naked. He climbed back to his spot and sat on the rock while daylight faded. He could stay here until he died of thirst. He could shoot himself in the head. He could climb higher on the hill and leap off the tunnel cut and land on the railroad track. No, no, and no. Beanpole owed him ten thousand dollars. He put on his clothes and walked back to his family in the darkness.

Jo was still resting. Unsure and awkward, Tucker stood beside her bed for several minutes, then leaned down to kiss her forehead. She awakened and hugged his neck. He patted her shoulder. She released him and he went downstairs and sat with Shiny on the porch, pointing out constellations. Shiny wanted to know the difference between stars and planets and moons.

"All the same, I reckon," Tucker said. "They're up there and we're down here. They ain't no roads either direction."

"At school they said a dog went up in space. A Russian dog."

"Communists are all dogs. They'll go anywhere. But they're afraid of folks in these hills."

"Is that what your gun's for? Communist dogs?"

"No. I got used to carrying one in Korea."

"Daddy, you been all over, ain't you."

"Mount Sterling twice. Once to Lexington. Where you been to, Shiny?"

"Morehead," Shiny said.

"Nowhere else?"

"Molton Holler. Lower Lick Creek. Bearskin Holler."

"Son, that's a big bunch more than I went to when I was your age. You're a regular traveling man."

"I ain't a man yet."

"No, but you will be."

Shiny scratched a swollen spot on his arm. It was red with a tiny dot in the middle.

"What's that," Tucker said.

"Hornet. They's a nest over the hill. Big as a basketball."

"Does it hurt?"

"Did when it bit me but not no more. Now it's just itchy."

"Let me see it."

Shiny offered his arm and Tucker moved to the porch light. The stinger was gone. Either it had never been in his arm or Shiny's body had already pushed it out.

"Your mom put anything on it?" Tucker said.

"No. I didn't tell her."

"Why not?"

"She told me to stay away from them. But I like how the nest looks."

"You best get to bed," Tucker said. "She'll have my hide if I keep you up late."

Shiny went upstairs and lay in bed, head turned to the window and the glimmer of stars. The house was quiet. He knew he'd remember this day the rest of his life. He'd driven a truck and his daddy was home.

On the porch Tucker lit a cigarette. Rhonda brought coffee for both of them and they sat in the darkness. She inhaled deeply, having missed his smell.

"Somebody's living in our old house," he said.

"Beanpole sold it. They say it looks nice."

"Work's been put to it."

"You mad at me?"

"No," he said. "It ain't your fault about them kids."

Rhonda closed her eyes and leaned against him, relieved. She'd feared this day since the state took the babies and now it was almost over.

"Where they got them living at?" Tucker said.

Rhonda went in the house and brought back copies of the forms she'd signed. Big Billy was at a medical facility in Frankfort and the girls lived in a group home in Lexington.

"We'll go see them," Tucker said.

"I'd like that."

"What'd the state people tell you?"

"Said the kids could get what they needed there. The right food and medicine. There's doctors for them."

"Anything else?"

"Said I wasn't working and you were in prison."

"Plenty of families like that."

"I told them," Rhonda said. "They said we didn't have the income to take care of them."

"Beanpole been giving you money?" he said.

"His wife ain't missed once. Forty a week. I didn't tell the state people. I've deviled myself wondering if I should've."

"No," Tucker said. "It's best you never. It'd make a bigger mess. Whole thing could have come out. Then I'd never get my money off him."

The Milky Way made a blizzard of stars in the narrow gap between the hills. A whip-poor-will called, its shrill sound close to the house.

"Where's the dogs?" Tucker said.

"Run off or died, one."

They sat, sipping coffee and talking as the night grew darker, the air chilled, and birdsong ceased. Occasionally Rhonda took a drag off Tucker's cigarette.

"How's Jo getting along?" he said.

"Tired. But she's glad you're back. Shiny, too."

"He's got a hornet bite on his arm."

"Big nest of them up the hill by the house. I ain't been able to get rid of them."

"I will," Tucker said. "I'm back now. I'll take care of things."

Within two hours he learned what had occurred in his absence. It amounted to very little—car wrecks, shootings, births and deaths, who got religion and who'd backslid. Abruptly he felt tired, as if the passage of time had accumulated in storage and flung itself over him. He was thirty years old and felt sixty. Did that mean at sixty he'd feel ninety, or would it be doubled to one hundred twenty? He pondered that, then asked Rhonda.

She giggled and they went inside and undressed in the bedroom. For a long time they lay side by side, both nervous but afraid of voicing fear. They slept. Dawn lifted the darkness to a veil of gray light imbued with birdsong. He caressed her and she stirred toward him, eyes opening in surprise. They touched each other slowly then rattled the bed as they always had, eradicating the years of terrible separation.

Chapter Thirteen

In the morning Shiny lay in bed with the sheets pulled tight to his chin. He remembered that his father was home and moved quietly across the narrow hall to Jo's room. She lay propped on several pillows, reading books lent by her teachers. They never gave Shiny books though he tried to do extra well in school so the state wouldn't take him away. He went downstairs to the kitchen.

Shiny was sitting on the edge of a wooden chair, eating an apple and drinking water, when he heard an unfamiliar tread and saw his father. Shiny stopped chewing, suddenly afraid without knowing why. He offered the apple. His father squinted at him, took the apple, and nibbled rapidly while holding two fingers behind his head like rabbit ears. Shiny laughed and they began duplicating various animals, copying their sounds and styles of eating. Tucker was snuffling the worn linoleum like a pig when Jo and Rhonda came into the room. Tucker reared back on his feet, still crouching, and crowed like a rooster until Jo smiled. He circled her like a cat, meowing and rubbing his body against her legs. Jo laughed and laughed.

Tucker stood. "You going to school today?" he said.

Jo looked at her mother.

"She might need a few days more," Rhonda said. "Best she lay on the couch and rest."

"Today is a house holiday," Tucker said. "Shiny stays home, too. We'll set and watch TV all day. But first I'll make some breakfast."

"No," Rhonda said. "I'll make breakfast. You can scrub potatoes and chop a few onions. Your idea of bacon is about like salty bark."

"Did you say bark?"

Tucker looked at his son and barked like a dog. Shiny began howling as if he were a beagle chasing a rabbit. After breakfast, Tucker repaired the flat tires on the car, re-gapped the spark plugs, cleaned the starter, and tightened the wires. He and Shiny drove to a garage and bought a new air filter. Shiny sat without talking and Tucker understood that the boy was more like him than he knew. On the way home, he stopped for a bottle of pop and drove to a wide place beside the creek. They sat in the shade of a willow with fronds long enough to drift in the ripples.

"Good place to fish," Tucker said. "You ever go?"

"No. I wanted to."

"But there wasn't nobody to take you, right?"

Shiny nodded.

"Well, I'm back now. We'll get you a rod and reel, hunt us up some nightcrawlers, and I'll teach you how."

"Is it hard?"

"Nope. Hard part's getting the hook out of the fish. It's easy to cut your hand. But I'll show you how. There's a trick to it."

Shiny nodded. He finished his bottle of pop and tossed it into the creek. They watched it get hung on a tree root and slowly fill with water. Tucker threw a rock at it, deliberately missing.

"You try," he said.

Shiny hurled a rock that went wide. He picked up another one.

"Here," Tucker said, "give this one a shot."

He handed his son a rock.

"Is it a special one?" Shiny said.

"Not really. But some are better for throwing. You want one that's kindly round-shaped, like a baseball but not as big. It'll go straight. Heavy is better than light, too. You don't want it to veer off."

Shiny's throw came closer to the bottle. He searched for rocks similar to the one his father had given him. After six more tries, he hit the bottle, and laughed.

"You know a lot, Daddy," he said.

"I listen and watch, same as you."

"At school they said you was in a pen."

"I was."

"Like a hog pen?"

"No. It's short for penitentiary. But it was like a hog pen, only with walls instead of wire fence."

"Is it the same as prison?"

"Yes. Did the kids say that, too?"

Shiny nodded.

"They said only bad people are in prison."

"You worried that I'm bad?" Tucker said.

"No." Shiny's voice was quick and he looked away.

"Son, there's all kinds of people in the pen. Good and bad. Most are just unlucky."

"Which one was you?"

"I was a little bit of all three, so in between. Most people are."

"In between good and bad?"

"That's right."

"How can you be in between luck?"

"Everybody is most of the time. People don't know they're lucky till the bad luck comes along."

Shiny frowned and threw a rock.

"Why'd you go to the prison pen?" he said.

"They got me for selling beer."

"At the bootlegger?"

"You know about that?"

"It's on the county line. A lot of the kids' daddies go over there."

"They talk about that in first grade?" Tucker said.

"I'm in second."

"Oh. Well, right. You're not a first-grader anymore. And I'm not in prison in anymore. We're right here."

"Are you going to stay?"

"Yes."

"Are you sure?"

"I still yet got to take you fishing. And there's more to learn about rocks. You ever hear of skipping one across water?"

"No."

"That'll be next. We need a wider creek. Or a pond."

"I know where there's a pond supposed to be at."

Tucker nodded and went to the car. Shiny followed him, trying to copy the way his father walked, the tilt of his shoulders. They drove home and spent the rest of the day drowsing in the front room, watching TV with a fuzzy black-and-white picture. Shiny asked why the commercials were for places in West Virginia.

"We're so far back in the hills," Tucker said, "we get TV from out of state."

Encouraged, Shiny asked dozens of questions that his father patiently answered. Rhonda's favorite soap opera came on and she made everyone hush. The reception began to fade. Tucker went outside to turn the antennae attached to a pole until the picture improved. The sound faded to a hum. Shiny stood in the door and relayed information between his father and mother. Rhonda said she'd rather hear what the people were saying because she already knew what they looked like. Tucker adjusted the antennae again to retrieve the sound. A hornet veered past him, a sentry, and he wondered how far the nest was from the house.

Later, when a cowboy show came on, Tucker switched reception to a good picture, explaining that what they said never mattered, but you had to know the color of each man's hat. At the end, the cowboy in the white hat always won.

"My hat's green," Shiny said. "What color is yours, Daddy?"

"Never much wore one. My hair's thick enough to shed water. About like a duck."

"But if you did, what color would it be?"

"Reckon I'd go with green, same as you."

The answer satisfied the boy, filling him with a sense of pride. He asked more questions until Rhonda shushed him.

Jo felt a little better but was still tired. She felt grateful that her father was home, though she wished he were seeing her at her best. She worried that her best was behind her now. A future of being fat and achy seemed awful. Her mother said it meant she was on her way to having kids of her own, and Jo kept that thought in place.

After the kids went to bed, Rhonda joined Tucker on the porch. The air had cooled enough for her to wear a sweater. They drank weak coffee, watching shadows join to form the night. During his time in prison she'd tried to trace the route that led to her situation, and in doing so wound up blaming everyone: her father for dying, Uncle Boot for his selfish desire, Tucker for showing up when he did, the state for taking her kids, Beanpole for sending her husband to the pen. Mainly she blamed herself for not fighting hard enough to protect her children.

"Honey," Tucker said.

"Say it again. You ain't called me that in a long while."

"Honey pie. Honey cake."

"I missed you," she said.

"I'm sorry I was gone so long."

"Why were you?"

"Had some trouble inside," he said.

"What kind?"

"You seen them scars on my chest and back?"

Rhonda nodded.

"That kind," he said.

"Couldn't you let it go?"

"In the pen, there ain't nowhere to let stuff go to. I'm back now."

"I'm glad of it," she said. "I wish I had my babies back, too."

"I been thinking on it. We can try."

"How?"

"Build an extra room on the side. Buy some fancy hospital beds. Get whatever it is they say we're needing for the kids. Medicine and whatnot."

"You really think so?" she said.

"Got to go see Beanpole first."

"About the money."

"Yep. Ten thousand bucks."

"Think it'll be enough?"

"With plenty extra."

Tree frogs made a chorus in the woods. A barn owl called, then another, as if in conversation. Orion lay sideways in the sky. Behind it the far stars blurred together like woven mist.

Chapter Fourteen

Beanpole's foray into snake-killing dogs had ended when a copperhead with a particularly potent poison bit the eight best dogs. Four died and he shot all the snakes. The next day he gave away the rest of the dogs. It was the lowest point of Beanpole's life. Disconsolate for weeks, he drank beer and ate cupcakes.

He watched the TV news every night. Politicians sent more and more soldiers to Vietnam, which cut into his bootlegging business. Some of the younger men liked marijuana, and he thought it was worth looking into. During World War II the government had grown hemp in Kentucky due to the ideal soil. That presented another problem—he wasn't a farmer but he wasn't much of a snake dog breeder either. Planting seeds had to be easier.

Every week Beanpole's sisters criticized him for not helping Jimmy more. It seemed to Beanpole that half his life happened when he wasn't around—family getting mad at him no matter where he was. He was afraid of women—of disappointing them and receiving their subsequent ire. A woman's anger made him feel worthless. The best strategy was to stay outdoors and give them whatever they wanted. The problem was he didn't know what they wanted. The only technique that always worked was offering sympathy and aspirin.

Jimmy was more trouble than snake dogs, with no reward in sight. He clamored to "move up" as he put it, like bootlegging was a grocery store where you started out as stock boy and eventually became the manager. Every time Beanpole gave him a hand, Jimmy grabbed a foot. His report on Tucker didn't help. Beanpole knew the two of them wouldn't get along but was surprised by Jimmy's outrage. He'd hoped that some time spent with Tucker would benefit the boy, provide him with a better example than his no-count daddy. Instead, it invigorated Jimmy's ambitions.

Beanpole considered giving him a task he was guaranteed to fail—maybe a run to Ohio along a route that was well known to the law. He could put Jimmy in the bootlegger shack, then pay the sheriff to arrest him. Beanpole chuckled to himself. He and the sheriff had been friends since childhood, and he relished the idea of bribing the sheriff to raid the very place he'd bribed him not to raid. They'd have a good laugh over that. But word would get out, and Beanpole would look bad—as if he couldn't protect his own nephew. Another option was waiting for Jimmy to follow his own path toward trouble, but that might take a while. With any luck Jimmy would get drafted. Maybe Beanpole would suggest he volunteer for Vietnam.

That afternoon Beanpole heard the sound of an unfamiliar vehicle coming around the ridge. The car came into view, listing to one side like a boat taking in water, moving steadily. Its back end rose in the air with every revolution of the wheels, indicating a spare tire that didn't match the rest. The driver honked the horn and stepped out. Beanpole set aside the shotgun and walked onto the porch.

Tucker approached slowly, surprised at the lack of dogs. The house was brick and clapboard with a wide porch that wrapped around the side facing over the hill. That area was screened and held a swing, a round metal table, and a few chairs. Beanpole stood at the top of the brick steps.

"Hidy," Beanpole said. "Come on up and set a spell."

Tucker nodded and climbed the steps and sat in a metal chair.

"You look good," Beanpole said.

Tucker nodded.

"Me," Beanpole said, "I got bigger. I know this looks like my belly but it ain't. It's table muscle."

He laughed, cutting it short when Tucker didn't change expression.

"Your wife home?" Tucker said.

"No, she's off running the roads to see her grandbabies."

"Quiet without them dogs," Tucker said.

"Didn't work out," Beanpole said. "I did get me an idea here lately. A snake bites you and it swells up, then goes back down, right?"

Tucker nodded.

"I been thinking the same thing might happen with a stick of wood. You trick a snake into biting it. The stick swells up and you cut it up fast and build a shed. When the swelling goes away, the wood'll shrink. You got you the best birdhouse in the world. Man could make good money selling them."

Tucker lit a cigarette and smoked it left-handed to keep his gun hand free. A lot could happen in five years and Beanpole might have gone softheaded. A butterfly drifted the hawkweed that speckled the edge of the yard.

"Jimmy said he brought you home," Beanpole said.

"Talks too much."

"He can drive."

"That boy couldn't drive a wedge up a goat's ass."

"Don't reckon you'd care to take him under your wing, teach him a few things, would you."

"Why would I do that?" Tucker said.

"Save me some trouble. Maybe save him some big trouble."

"He'll kill somebody or get killed, one."

"He'd be all right if a man was to stretch a cow pussy over his head and let a bull fuck some sense into him."

"Be pretty tough on the cow."

"It ain't about the cow," Beanpole said. "I'm talking about Jimmy."

"What you ain't talking about is money."

Beanpole's tension eased off now that he didn't have to bring up what promised to be a hard conversation. The best way was direct and pragmatic. Tucker was too smart to be hoodwinked. Beanpole knew what happened to men who underestimated Tucker.

"Heard you had some trouble in the pen," Beanpole said.

"Motor-sickle gang out of Dayton."

"Them Satans ain't nobody to fool with. They'll carry a grudge."

"I found that out."

"You square it with them?"

"Not exactly."

"Then how'd you leave it?"

"Gave them more grudges than they wanted to carry."

Beanpole laughed. The sound trickled away in the still air. A woodpecker battered a tree, and the first cicada of the day began its distant sound.

"What I heard," Beanpole said, "you put them bikers down and got extra time tacked on for it."

"That's about right," Tucker said.

"I know it's tough inside."

"No, you don't. You pay men to find out for you."

"Them extra months was your doing, not mine."

"The Satans knew your name. They knew I run shine for you. Said you were the reason they came at me. One of your men up in Ohio snitched five or six of them out. They was trying to get back at you through me."

"You believed a bunch of buckeye bikers?" Beanpole said.

"I did after they tried to kill me three times."

"Three times?"

"La Grange and Eddyville, both."

"Satans locked up everywhere, I guess."

"They ain't why I'm here."

Beanpole waited for him to continue but Tucker sat in the chair, his off-colored eyes steady, never blinking. He could have been a lizard for all the lack of motion. Beanpole understood that Tucker could outwait him. He'd had years of practice.

"Your wife," Beanpole said, "got forty dollars a week. Like we agreed. Never missed once. Angela dropped it off."

"Rhonda told me."

"Five and half years I done that. Forty bucks a week is eleven thousand, four hundred and forty dollars."

"I don't need you to cipher numbers for me."

"I'm trying to lay it all out so we both know what we're talking about."

Tucker could see where this was headed. When it came to money, Beanpole was tight as the end of a woodpile. The air stilled and a swift rain arrived, the drops making clumps of fescue quiver in the yard. It passed fast. The slab of sky lightened between the hills. Rain released the scent of cedar drifting from the tree line.

"How much did you make selling my house?" Tucker said.

"Ain't got nothing to do with it."

"It was my house."

"You sold it to me. What I done with it is my business. You can sell my old one if you've a mind to. Don't bother me one whit."

"I might do that, but I ain't got a place to live if I do."

"Nothing's easy."

"Living in the pen ain't either."

"You're out. Your family got took care of."

"I got a record now," Tucker said. "Ain't a whole lot of places will hire me."

"What kind of job you aiming to get?"

"The kind where a man gets paid what he's owed."

Beanpole didn't think Tucker would do anything at his house, but he'd seen men get pretzeled up from prison. Nobody came out better off.

"Way I see it," Beanpole said, "that extra time ate up the ten thousand and then some. But I'm game to let that go."

"Let what go?"

"You don't owe me the extra."

"What extra is that?"

"Fourteen hundred and forty dollars."

"I got arrested and went away for you. I lost my house, a car, and four of my kids. Now you're saying I owe you money?"

"I'm sorry about those kids. But that ain't got nothing to do with me."

"If I'd been there," Tucker said, "it would have gone different."

"If you'd been there, you might've done something that got you put in prison."

"You're saying being inside kept me from getting locked up?"

"That's why you agreed in the first place. So the cops couldn't get you on that Salt Lick thing. I helped you then. I helped your wife when I didn't have to."

"Did she ask for help? No. Did I ask you? No. We made a deal. I want my ten thousand. I aim to get my kids back with it."

"The state don't work that way. Ain't like prison where they get out and go home. You'll not get those kids back."

"How do you know?"

"My wife's second cousin had a kid got took by the state. I gave her money for lawyers, run her up to Frankfort, and went to court. Did everything we could. Judge said the kid was better off. Maybe yours are, too."

Tucker felt separate from himself, as if he were watching the two of them talk on the porch. Time was moving slowly, the way it had during combat in Korea and the knife fight at LaGrange. He recognized it as a bad sign, especially here on Beanpole's porch in daylight with his car parked in the yard and Beanpole's wife coming home any time. He stood, his movement slow and torpid as a snake in spring.

Beanpole understood that he had no advantage whatsoever. Tucker was the most dangerous when he appeared benign, moving like a man stunned by heat. He'd made an error that might cost him everything. He shouldn't have mentioned Tucker's kids.

"Don't run off," Beanpole said. "Let's talk this through."

"We done did."

"Now, no. There's a way out."

"My babies got took while I was serving time for you. And you sit there saying they're better off for it."

"I didn't say that," Beanpole said. "I'm trying to help you."

"I never asked for help my whole life. I want what I'm owed."

"We can work something out."

"Ten thousand dollars."

Beanpole didn't move or speak. Tucker walked down the steps. At his car he turned and looked at Beanpole for a long time, then lifted his hand. He drove out the ridge and off the hill, wondering why he'd waved. It was instinctive, as if something had ended, a farewell to everything that had happened between them for the past sixteen years.

Beanpole watched the dust settle onto low-hanging leaves, heard the engine whining in first gear down the slope. He was disappointed with himself and the result. He'd figured on offering five thousand cash and calling it even, but things got out of hand too fast. The air turned quiet.

Now he had two problems—Jimmy and Tucker. They couldn't be more different as men, but they presented the same difficulty. Neither was controllable. Beanpole sat without moving for an hour, examining options, sorting through potential outcomes and further problems. Every approach was flawed and led circuitously back to the primary situation: Tucker had transformed into an enemy and Jimmy was a liability. An hour later he figured out what to do.

Chapter Fifteen

The next day Tucker removed his weapons from the closet where he'd hidden them six years before. On the porch he cleaned the pistol and reassembled it, thinking about the conversation with Beanpole. It didn't go the way Tucker wanted, and he doubted that Beanpole had liked it either. He could see both perspectives but it didn't matter anymore. Beanpole would send a man to kill him. The smart move would be to bring someone in from Dayton and pin the murder on the motorcycle gang. That would take a couple of weeks to set up and Tucker didn't believe Beanpole would wait. He'd want to kill Tucker soon, before Tucker came after him.

He was sharpening the Ka-Bar knife when Rhonda joined him.

"Shiny got in them hornets again," she said. "I can't make him quit."

"I'll take care of it."

"He won't listen."

"I didn't either when I was a kid. You know what my mother said about me and my brothers? One boy is a boy. Two is half a boy. And three ain't a boy at all."

"What does that mean?" Rhonda said.

"I don't know. She said it is all."

She watched him whet the knife on the stone. He spat on his arm for lather and shaved a patch of hair, then went back to sharpening. He crossed his legs and stropped the blade on his boot heel.

"Ain't seen that knife in a while," Rhonda said.

"I got one last little bit of trouble to take care of."

"With Beanpole?"

He didn't answer. He'd done enough to muddy her life and he needed to walk the mud hole dry, not make it deeper. The more she knew, the worse she'd worry. War and prison had taught him that sides didn't really exist, that everyone was eventually caught in the middle of something. At least he could put off Rhonda's turn for a while.

"Where's that hornet nest at?" he said.

"Up the hill past the blackberry bushes. Watch yourself. It's bad to be snaky in there."

"I don't mind snakes."

"I remember you eating one once."

"Yep," he said. "Breakfast the day I met you."

"Let's lay down a minute."

They went inside and rested in their bedroom. The midday light slid through the window. Tucker watched it, thinking about the thousands of hours he'd spent in a cell with no window. He wondered if this had been Beanpole's bedroom, if he'd lain here watching the same light.

He touched Rhonda's shoulder and spoke.

"Ever miss our old house?"

"Every day."

"It was littler."

"It was ours," she said. "It's where the kids were born."

"Maybe we can buy it back."

"I'd like that."

Later, Tucker sharpened a bucksaw and put it in a gunnysack along with several strands of wire, work gloves, and a roll of duct tape. He wore two sets of clothes with a loose layer on the outside, his pants tucked into his boots. Armed with pistol and knife, he walked down the hill at an angle. Milkweed swayed along the edge of a rain gully. Tucker sweated heavily inside his double layer of clothing. He circled the blackberry bushes, squatted, and waited, listening intently. Twice he stood to relieve the ache in his knees, and settled back to his patient crouch.

He heard the hornet before he saw it, then watched it circle and land. It was nearly an inch long with white and black markings on its face. The hornet rose from a blossom and flew low through the woods. Tucker followed its direct path up the slanting land to a blue beech. Hanging beneath a low bough was a nest the shape of a giant lightbulb. He watched four hornets come out of a hole near the bottom of the nest and fly into the woods. Another one buzzed close, veering away and returning in tight aerial arcs.

Tucker opened the gunnysack and removed the bucksaw and duct tape. He tore off a short piece of tape and fastened a corner to his left sleeve, leaving most of the sticky side free. He slid the gloves over his hands and hung the bucksaw on the crook of his elbow. A hornet landed on his leg and another on his arm but he ignored them. He approached the nest slowly to avoid disturbing the air, and in one quick motion sealed the entry hole with the strip of duct tape. He lifted the gunnysack around the nest and tied it to the branch. Disturbed, the trapped hornets increased their buzzing until the gunnysack seemed to vibrate. He used the bucksaw to cut the limb off the tree. He lowered the bag to the ground, looped wire around the cloth, and tightened it around the sawed branch.

Tucker walked swiftly down the hill, using the branch as a handle to carry the enclosed nest. A few hornets followed him. One found the exposed skin of his neck and he slapped at it, feeling the sharp sting just before killing the hornet. Safely away from the tree, he stopped and killed three more. His neck felt burned by fire. He removed his gloves and prodded the swollen area, resisting the urge to scratch. He carried the nest up the hill, seeking a ridge path at the top. His plan was to tie it to a tree beside the old fire road built by the Forest Service. Hornets had a right to live.

At the top of the ridge he rested, then removed the top layer of clothing. His body immediately cooled. He buttoned the shirt to make a pouch for the extra pants and gloves, tied the sleeves together, and slung the makeshift ruck over his shoulder. With his weapons back in place, he began walking the ridge toward the gully where he intended to leave the nest. Wind in the high boughs brushed leaves like the sound of distant water. As the canopy shifted, light flowed across the forest floor. He'd forgotten the pleasures of being in the woods. Now that his main purpose was accomplished, he could enjoy the walk, the sense of freedom. A dove called, then a crow. He figured the crow was warning deer that a human was near, and assumed it was himself until Jimmy stepped around a tree with a pistol.

Tucker immediately began assessing the situation, his mind skipping from actions to outcomes. He kept returning to the single unassailable fact—he'd let his guard down.

Jimmy adjusted the Borsalino hat as if reminding Tucker of it, and spoke.

"You ain't hunting dryland fish with a bucksaw."

"No, I ain't."

"What's in the bag?"

"Bees."

"I knowed some boys to flavor liquor with honey."

Sunlight sifted through the tangled tree limbs overhead. A cicada began its complex clicking song, the sound coming from the west. Tucker shifted his weight. He'd made the error of overburdening his gun hand with the hornet nest. He could shoot left-handed but the pistol was on his right hip, and he was too far away to use the knife. He could force Jimmy into making a mistake or wait for him to do it on his own. Neither was a good option.

"Reckon you got the drop on me, Jimmy. I didn't hear you."

"Heel taps don't make noise in the woods."

Irritated hornets rattled the nest, making the gunnysack shake. Jimmy gestured with his pistol, a thirty-eight revolver.

"Set that bucksaw down," he said.

Tucker dropped it. Jimmy nodded.

"You got a pistol on you?"

"Yep."

"Take it out slow and turn loose of it. Don't get no big ideas."

Tucker lifted the pistol from his back pocket and let it fall to the ground.

"You're the boss, Jimmy."

"Yes, I am. I'm the boss. Sure different than driving you all over the countryside, you telling me what to do."

"I hear Beanpole's getting out of snake dogs."

"I'm glad," Jimmy said, "Them dogs barked for a living. That racket got on my last nerve."

Tucker shook the sack. The hornets responded with fury, producing a hum of a higher frequency than before.

"I could cut you into the honey business," Tucker said. "You ort to see this honeycomb. I'll get fifty dollars for it."

"Ain't no honeycomb worth that much."

Tucker switched the branch to his other hand, and turned sideways to hide the knife on his belt. He slowly drew it from its scabbard, out of Jimmy's sight.

"Don't set them loose," Jimmy said.

"I smoked them down. They can't hardly fly."

"What kind are they?"

Tucker lifted the knife concealed by his body. In a swift motion he slit the gunnysack, threw it, and hurled himself sideways to the ground. The sack hit Jimmy in the chest. Angry hornets rushed from the bag, seeking an enemy, a black haze swirling around Jimmy's head. Jimmy moved backward, firing three wild shots, then turned and ran into the woods. Tucker retrieved his pistol, and followed.

Jimmy was easier to track than a rabbit in snow. The heels of his cowboy boots left deep imprints in the soft earth, the toes dragging dirt forward in triangles that aimed the direction he ran. Tucker passed bent tree limbs with leaves quivering from Jimmy's passage. A patch of trillium was crushed and scattered. Tucker stopped, cupping an ear forward with his free hand, hearing the intermittent rasp of labored breath. He walked with his pistol in front of him, approaching the sound. A Judas tree had a broken branch. Past it was a rain gully where Jimmy lay, breathing hard and groaning. He'd run into the tree, fallen, and lost his gun. Hornet stings webbed his face with welts. One eye was swollen shut. He held his right arm as if protecting it.

Tucker found Jimmy's gun and slipped it into his belt.

"Lucky you ain't allergic," Tucker said. "You'd be dead already."

"Yeah, I'm lucky as a dog with two dicks."

"I can dig them stingers out."

"No," Jimmy said. "Arm's worse."

"Broke?"

"I don't know. But it hurts worse than my face."

"Any get you in the mouth?"

Jimmy shook his head. Tucker turned away, sniffed the air, and walked toward the coolest area of the woods. He studied the weeds until finding wild parsley. Shredding several leaves from the stems, he wet them with water, and lay the pulp on the flat side of his canteen. He mashed the leaves with his blade. He walked back to Jimmy, who hadn't moved.

"Lay still," Tucker said. "This might hurt at first."

Very gently he daubed the parsley poultice on Jimmy's face. Jimmy squirmed, moaning low in his throat. Tucker held the back of his head to halt his struggle. After a few minutes Jimmy relaxed as the pain began to subside, soothed by the herb.

"Let me see your arm," Tucker said.

Jimmy tried to move but stopped, emitting a loud groan. Tucker squatted beside him, released the buttons of Jimmy's cuff, and slit the sleeve along his forearm. A lump the size of a walnut rose beneath the skin.

"Arm ain't bent," Tucker said. "That's good, means only one of the bones is broke."

"Only one?"

"There's two in there, Jimmy. Did you not know that?"

Jimmy shook his head. He was breathing through his mouth, trying to keep his good eye focused.

"I'll make a splint from hickory sticks," Tucker said.

"Where'd you learn all this at?"

"Army."

"You a medic?"

"No," Tucker said. "We all got a little training in it."

"To help each other?"

"To help the enemy."

"That don't make sense."

"If you got captured," Tucker said, "you were supposed to tell the enemy you were the medic. They might not kill you."

"Why not?"

"They needed docs, too," Tucker said. "Where's your car at?"

"Bottom of the fire road."

"Smart boy. Way I would have come in."

Tucker went back for his bucksaw, veering around the swarm of hornets that covered the nest and gunnysack. He sawed two chunks of hickory, green but still stiff enough to hold. He cut the rest of Jimmy's sleeve off, ripped several strips of cloth, and tied the hickory loosely on either side of his forearm. He poured water from his canteen on the strips.

"This'll be rough," he said.

He placed a knee on Jimmy's chest to stop any resistance, then cinched the wet cloth into tight knots. Jimmy moaned, twisting his head, beating Tucker with his good arm. Tucker ignored the flailing. After tying the splint he held the canteen to Jimmy's mouth. Water dribbled down his chin, sluicing a path through the parsley that speckled his face. A hornet drifted lazily by as if checking up on its work. Tucker swatted it from the air and stomped it.

"I got to take your shirt off and make a sling."

Jimmy nodded. Tucker helped him sit, unbuttoned the chambray shirt, and removed it. He fastened a sling with the body of the shirt holding the splinted arm. He lit a cigarette and handed it to Jimmy.

"All right, now," Tucker said. "Rest you a minute. And we'll get off this hillside."

"What're you doing this for?" Jimmy said.

"Helping you after you drawed down on me?"

Jimmy nodded.

"Way I figure it," Tucker said, "you were following Beanpole's orders. That about right?"

Jimmy nodded again.

"How much?" Tucker said.

"Huh?"

"How much was he paying you?"

"Five hundred. Plus he'd move me up. Boss over the stillers."

"You can't boss them people."

"Beanpole told me that."

"Five hundred," Tucker said. "Them damn Dayton Satans had a bigger bounty on me."

"Maybe I'll collect off them, too."

"That's a good sign. Making a joke."

Jimmy grinned, his good eye disappearing in the swollen folds of skin. Tucker almost felt sorry for the boy, shirtless, broken arm, face swelled up—and still trying to impress him. It was time to use that against him along with the resentment he'd noticed outside the prison.

"Beanpole say why he wanted me out of the way?"

"No."

"He owes me money," Tucker said. "Ten thousand for going to prison. Him not wanting to pay me is why you're sitting there banged up and stung."

Jimmy didn't answer.

"Think he'll give you five hundred now?" Tucker said.

"No."

"He can't use banks," Tucker said. "He keeps his money somewhere close. Where do you think it's at?"

"I don't know."

"You must have some idea on it."

"No, I don't."

"All right," Tucker said. "Think a minute. He's got to be able to get at it without no fuss. That means it ain't buried out back. He'd not hide it in an outbuilding either. What's that leave?"

"In the house somewhere."

"Is there a basement?"

"No. Concrete block foundation."

"Attic?"

"Don't have one."

"So it's inside," Tucker said. "He got a deep freeze for game?"

Jimmy shook his head.

"It's in the wall or floorboards, one."

Jimmy nodded.

"Where's his wife at?" Tucker said.

"Visiting grandbabies. He said to come by when I was done. Gave me three days to . . . You know."

"Yeah, I know. Finish the job. Let's you and me go get our money."

"I ain't stealing off my uncle."

"Me neither. But he ort to pay your doctor bills at least."

They sat for a minute. Tucker knew Jimmy didn't have a lot of choice—unarmed and hurt. He liked this side of Jimmy, not talking so much. The woods were dimming as the sun slid behind the western tree line. He wanted off the hill before dark.

Tucker helped Jimmy to his feet and headed out of the ridge. He found Jimmy's hat, dusted it off, and set it on his head. They moved slowly, Jimmy favoring one leg, his balance off-kilter with his arm in a sling. Tucker carried both guns. He walked behind Jimmy, steadying him on a steep bank, holding his good arm when they had to step over a gully. Pain made him docile. Travel was easier at the old fire road, a rutted lane down the hill that the state cleared every couple of years. By the time they reached Jimmy's car, full dark had enveloped them.

Tucker settled Jimmy in the passenger seat and drove. Jimmy leaned against the door, grunting at every bump in the road. Tucker didn't begrudge the boy for trying to shoot him down. What bothered him was Beanpole's sending Jimmy. Such a poor decision meant Beanpole was losing his edge. He should have offered to pay half what he owed. Tucker would have taken it and called them square.

He stopped at the foot of Beanpole's hill and put the Borsalino on his head. The hat was small and he tilted it low on his forehead. He pulled Jimmy until his body lay across the bench seat.

"Stay low," he said.

He rolled his window down and drove slowly up the hill. At the top, he honked his horn once, then eased along the driveway. Two windows held dim illumination from within. He parked in the grass at an angle to the house and flicked the headlights off and on twice. Jimmy groaned, trying to push himself up. Tucker struck him twice in the head with the pistol and Jimmy lay still. Blood trickled from a cut in his temple.

Tucker heard the front door of the house open, the squeal of the screen door. Beanpole's shadowy bulk blocked the light. Tucker tipped his head to let the hat's brim conceal his face. He held Jimmy's pistol below the open window.

"Jimmy," Beanpole said. "What'd I tell you about parking in the grass. My wife'll tear you up one side and down the other."

Tucker watched him silently. On the porch Beanpole blended into the darkness.

"Jimmy?" Beanpole said again.

Tucker emitted a low moan.

"He wing you?" Beanpole said. "Where's he at?"

Beanpole moved to the edge of the porch and down the plank steps. Light glinted off a revolver in his hand.

"Jimmy?" he said, lifting the gun. "Who is that?"

Tucker raised his arm and fired through the open window, aiming low. Beanpole gasped and staggered. He grabbed for the step railing but missed and fell. Tucker opened the car door and approached him. Blood spread on Beanpole's pants, already being absorbed by the dirt. It was a leg wound, not too bad.

Tucker picked up Beanpole's pistol, a Colt forty-five, and aimed both guns at him.

"Anybody home?" Tucker said.

"No," Beanpole said. "Just me."

"Where's the money at?"

"In the house. Help me up and we'll get it."

"Tell me where you got it hid."

"Nope."

"I won't take more than what you're owing me."

"Damn it all to hell," Beanpole said. "Why'd you have to shoot me?"

"Where's the money at, Beanpole?"

"Ten thousand and not a nickel more."

"You got my word on that."

"Staircase. Under the second step. Jiggle it from the right, then pull hard. It'll come right up."

"All right," Tucker said. "Don't go nowhere."

"Fuck you."

In the house Tucker turned on the light and knelt before the steps. The tread shifted beneath his grip, then pulled away. Inside the alcove were stacks of bills, dozens of them wrapped in rubber bands. He counted out ten thousand dollars in fifties, twenties, and tens, and put it in his pocket. He went outside.

Beanpole lay on his back, breathing hard, holding his thigh. Tucker removed the bundle of money from his pocket.

"You want to count it?" he said.

"No, I trust you," Beanpole said.

Tucker put the cash away and withdrew Jimmy's gun.

"Now what," Beanpole said.

"You shouldn't have put that boy on me," Tucker said.

He shot Beanpole four times in the chest with Jimmy's gun. In the house he gathered the rest of the money and carried it outside. Jimmy lay across the bench seat, still breathing. Tucker dragged him behind the steering wheel. He removed the sling and cut the splint away, then placed the cash on the seat beside him. He tossed the Borsalino on the floorboards and opened the driver-side door. He walked back to the porch steps. Using Beanpole's forty-five, he shot Jimmy twice, and dropped the gun beside Beanpole.

He wrapped Jimmy's hand around his thirty-eight and set it in his lap. The guns were two different calibers, which would help the law put things together. Tucker didn't figure they'd worry too much about a gunfight in a bootlegger family. The blood-splashed money tied it all up. The sheriff would figure if another man was involved, he'd have taken the cash. Nothing tracked back to Tucker.

He walked to the edge of the yard and climbed the hill at an angle. The sky was clear. Moonlight illuminated the top of the hill and he followed the ridge as if it were a road, circling three hollers, two creeks, and a dry rain branch. He dropped down the hill for a shortcut past a blackberry thicket and into an open field. A great horned owl proclaimed its hunting territory, and the night sounds momentarily stilled. A slight motion in the field ahead of him caused him to freeze, then squat and peer through the tops of the weeds. He saw a white figure and wondered if it was a ghost. He'd never seen one before. Depending on who it was, he might not mind too much. Still, it was disconcerting.

The ghost came straight toward him, unerring in its aim. He stood to confront it, unafraid but aware of a sudden sweat on his skin in the cool night air. It wasn't a ghost but a woman in a white nightgown. Long gray hair hung like a shawl past her shoulders. He waited for her to stop, to acknowledge his presence, but she maintained her slow walk, and in the dim light he recognized Zeph's mother. Tucker underwent relief. Beulah had been blind for years and couldn't identify him to the sheriff.

Beulah moved close to him, lifted her arm slowly, and touched the side of his face. Her palm was soft. She stroked his brow, the curve of his eye sockets, his nose.

"You're a Tucker," she said. "Third boy of Sarah. I fetched you into the world."

"Yes, ma'am," he said.

"And your first child, too," she said.

"Billy."

"His head was swelled up. I didn't know what to do. I was afraid it would kill the mother and I took care of her instead of the boy."

"He lived," Tucker said.

"I heard. But he wasn't right. I'm sorry."

"It wasn't your fault," he said.

"I went blind after that. God's punishment. I never grannied another baby."

She lowered her hand, then her head as if looking at the earth with her filmy eyes. He wondered if she smelled the cordite from the gunfire on his clothes. If so, she could put him in jail.

"What are you doing out here?" he said.

"I get restless of the night."

Her house was half a mile away, across the field and down a slope at the end of a lower ridge. It had been his favorite spot as a child. In summer Tucker visited her house for a drink of water. He couldn't leave her alone and he couldn't kill her.

"Let me get you home," he said.

"You're in trouble aren't you," she said.

"Not if nobody knows where I am."

"I can't see anyone."

"No, but you know me. That's enough for the law."

"I never been one to favor laws."

She turned and he followed her across the field. A breeze set the sedge in motion like ripples in a pond. A thin cloud crossed the moon, turning the night into translucent gauze, but she continued her slow pace as if she could see as well as him. They walked along a path to a dirt road that ended at the squared-off shadow of a house. He watched her move to the dark porch, heard the door open and close.

Tucker walked back across the field, trying to imagine being blind. Day and night would be the same except for the temperature of the air. He shivered involuntarily. Maybe they'd each seen a ghost.

He abandoned his shortcut and climbed the land. At the top of the hill he headed east along the ridge, following the stars. He'd be home in time for breakfast with his family.

Epilogue

Beulah told no one about meeting Tucker in the woods, not even her son. She died in her sleep at age one hundred one or one hundred three.

Zeph quit working at the grade school after his mother died. Every year he gathered morels and ginseng, which he sold at a profit. He had a heart attack in the woods and died listening to birds, looking at the sky, happy.

Jimmy was buried in the family cemetery. Two women claimed to have had his children. One child became the first woman deputy sheriff in Rowan County. The other, a boy, moved to Texas and was never heard from again.

Angela lived with her youngest daughter and was happier than her family remembered. She never spoke of Beanpole, although some nights alone on the porch she recalled the early days of their courtship.

Uncle Boot served as deputy sheriff for six years, then ran successfully for sheriff. After twenty-two years he retired and opened a small boat rental business on the newly formed Cave Run Reservoir.

Mr. Howorth died under mysterious circumstances at his hardware store. Despite no alibi, Mrs. Howorth was exonerated, and her husband's death was deemed an accident. She dyed her hair, moved to Florida, and claimed to be from Tennessee.

After the theft of his pistol, Tom Freeman never picked up a hitchhiker again. He sold products for Procter & Gamble, switched to life insurance, then real estate. He retired at age fifty-five, a millionaire thrice over.

Hattie never revealed the facts of Marvin's death. She moved to Chicago and formed a loving relationship with a woman. She joined the Daughters of Bilitis, an early gay rights group, and became a prominent organizer. In 1970, she marched in Chicago's first Gay Pride parade.

Jo received an academic scholarship to Morehead State University. She became a special education teacher in Carter County. She married a logger and had three children, all with full cognitive abilities.

Shiny joined the army and thrived within its structure. After twenty years he retired and returned to the hills with his third wife and a young child. He supplemented his military pension by repairing chainsaws and lawn mowers.

Rhonda's attempts to regain custody of her children failed. She visited them once a month. Her recovery from depression was gradual but complete, and she remained in love with Tucker throughout her days.

Ida and Velmey died young when influenza swept through the shared bedroom of the care facility, taking eleven children. Bessie was transferred to a newer institution in Frankfort, where she worked in the kitchen.

Big Billy became a favorite of the nursing staff. He learned to communicate through a series of grunts, and smiled often. At age sixty-one he died of a stroke. His funeral was well attended.

Tucker bought his old house and returned to it. A few years later he replaced Zeph as the janitor at the elementary school. He never used his weapons again.

Acknowledgments

For editorial assistance during the writing of this book, I am very grateful to Amy Hundley, Nicole Aragi, Jonathan Lethem, James Offutt, Kathi Whitley, Levi Henriksen, and Melissa Allee Ginsburg.

For financial assistance, I thank the Ucross Foundation, the Mississippi Arts Commission, and the University of Mississippi.